SOMEWHERE IN ARIZONA.

ALL RIGHT, CUPCAKES. *LISTEN UP!*

YOU'RE ABOUT TO SEE THE GRAND CANYON. TRY NOT TO *BREAK* IT. AND IF ANY OF YOU CAUSES ANY *TROUBLE* ON THIS FIELD TRIP--

--I WILL *PERSONALLY* SEND YOU BACK TO CAMPUS THE *HARD* WAY!

~yawn~

WELCOME BACK, SLEEPYHEAD.

UM, I DON'T...

JASON? YOU OKAY?

HEY, PIPER, HOW'S IT FEEL TO BE BACK ON THE *REZ*? INSTEAD OF A SECRET HANDSHAKE, DO YOU ALL DO A *RAIN DANCE* OR SOMETHING?

THIS IS HUALAPAI LAND. MY DAD IS *CHEROKEE*.

OF COURSE, YOU'D NEED A FEW *BRAIN CELLS* TO KNOW THE DIFFERENCE.

SO WAS YOUR *MOM* IN THIS TRIBE? OH, THAT'S RIGHT; YOU NEVER KNEW YOUR MOM.

SEE YA, *SACAGAWEA*.

TAKE IT EASY, BABE. YOU'RE WITH ME.

WHAT COULD BE BETTER?

WIND IS PICKING UP. CHECK THIS OUT.

WOULD'VE BEEN COOLER IF I HAD SOME RUBBER BANDS.

HOW'D WE MEET, ANYWAY? I MEAN, IF WE'RE SUCH GOOD FRIENDS.

IT WAS...

YOU KNOW, I DON'T RECALL EXACTLY.

BUT I'M *ADHD*. I CAN'T BE EXPECTED TO REMEMBER DETAILS.

GOT SOME CLOUDS MOVING IN.

BLONDIE! FRONT AND CENTER!

I'LL, UH, BE RIGHT BACK.

IMPOSSIBLE. THAT LIGHTNING WOULD'VE KILLED *TWENTY* MEN.

WHATEVER. THERE'S MORE THAN ONE WAY TO *KILL* A DEMIGOD.

WHOA!

-UHHN-

WHOOSH

GUYS! A LITTLE *HELP?!*

I HOPE YOU'RE GOOD, KID. HOLD THEM OFF WHILE I GO AFTER VALDEZ.

HOLD THEM OFF? *HOW?*

TRUST YOUR INSTINCTS!

HANG ON, CUPCAKE!

WHERE IS HE?

WHERE'S WHO?

COACH HEDGE? HE GOT CARRIED AWAY BY SOME *TORNADO* DUDES.

THEY WERE STORM SPIRITS. *VENTI.* DON'T ASK HOW I KNOW THAT, BECAUSE I HAVE *NO IDEA.*

YOU MEAN *ANEMOI THUELLAI.* THAT'S THE GREEK TERM.

ARE YOU THE ONLY HALF-BLOODS HERE? IS THERE *NO ONE* ELSE?

UM, JUST US.

NO, NO, *NO!* SHE TOLD ME IF I CAME HERE, I'D FIND THE ANSWER. I'VE BEEN *TRICKED!*

ANNABETH, WE GOTTA SPLIT. THOSE STORM SPIRITS MIGHT COME BACK. LET'S GET THESE THREE TO CAMP AND FIGURE IT OUT THERE.

FINE!

I'M NOT GOING ANYWHERE WITH HER. SHE LOOKS LIKE SHE WANTS TO *KILL* ME!

SHE'S COOL. IT'S JUST THAT HER BOYFRIEND--A GUY NAMED *PERCY JACKSON*--WENT MISSING THREE DAYS AGO, AND SHE WAS TOLD SHE'D FIND HIM HERE.

NOW COME ON. WE'LL TAKE YOU SOMEPLACE SAFE.

WHEREVER THEY'RE GOING, IT CAN'T BE WORSE THAN THE WILDERNESS SCHOOL.

WHO ARE YOU GUYS?

HALF-BLOODS. LIKE YOU.

I'VE BEEN CALLED "HALF-BLOOD" BEFORE, AND IT WASN'T MEANT AS A *COMPLIMENT*.

SHE MEANS WE'RE DEMIGODS. HALF MORTAL, HALF *GOD*.

YOU SEEM TO KNOW A LOT.

MY NAME IS ANNABETH. MY MOM IS *ATHENA*, GODDESS OF WISDOM. BUTCH IS A SON OF *IRIS*, THE RAINBOW GODDESS.

HYAH!

THIS. IS. *CRAZY.*

EVERYBODY HANG ON TO SOMETHING!

HERE WE GO!

WELCOME TO *CAMP HALF-BLOOD*, GANG.

IF THIS IS ANOTHER BOARDING SCHOOL, I MAY ACTUALLY *LIKE* IT HERE.

THESE ARE THE ONES? WAY OLDER THAN THIRTEEN.

ANY SIGN OF PERCY?

NO.

I HOPE THEY'RE WORTH THE TROUBLE. BECAUSE *THESE TWO* SURE DON'T LOOK IT.

GEE, THANKS. WHAT ARE WE, YOUR NEW PETS?

THIS ONE, ON THE OTHER HAND... THIS ONE HAS *PROMISE*.

ALL DEMIGODS ARE WORTH SAVING, DREW. TRY TO MAKE OUR NEW ARRIVALS FEEL *WELCOME*.

THEY'LL NEED A TOUR OF CAMP. HOPEFULLY BY THE CAMPFIRE TONIGHT, THEY'LL BE CLAIMED.

"CLAIMED"? SO WE'RE NOT PETS. MORE LIKE WE'RE IN THE *LOST AND FOUND*.

SOMETHING LIKE THAT.

WHEN A HALF-BLOOD IS CLAIMED, IT MEANS--

WELL, IT MEANS *THAT*.

WHY IS EVERYONE--?

AH!

IS MY HAIR ON FIRE?

LEO, YOU'VE JUST BEEN CLAIMED BY *HEPHAESTUS*, THE GOD OF BLACKSMITHS AND FORGES. IT MEANS HE'S YOUR DAD.

WHO? THE GOD OF WHAT?

THIS *CAN'T* BE GOOD. THE *CURSE*...

NOT NOW, BUTCH.

WILL, GIVE LEO THE TOUR AND INTRODUCE HIM TO HIS BUNKMATES IN CABIN NINE.

LET'S GO, *HAMMERHEAD.*

I THOUGHT THE GOD OF BLACKSMITHS WAS NAMED "VULCAN."

THAT'S HIS *ROMAN* NAME.

WHAT'S THAT ON YOUR RIGHT ARM, JASON?

STRANGE...

I'VE NEVER SEEN MARKINGS LIKE THIS. THEY LOOK LIKE THEY WERE *BURNED* INTO YOUR SKIN. WHERE DID YOU GET THEM?

I'M GETTING REALLY TIRED OF SAYING THIS, BUT I DON'T KNOW.

THEN YOU NEED TO GO STRAIGHT TO CHIRON.

DREW, WOULD YOU--?

ABSOLUTELY.

THIS WAY, *SWEETIE.* I'LL INTRODUCE YOU TO THE CAMP DIRECTOR.

HE'S AN... INTERESTING GUY.

WHO'S CHIRON? IS JASON IN SOME KIND OF TROUBLE?

GOOD QUESTION. COME ON, WE NEED TO TALK.

I HAVE TO SAY, YOU'RE TAKING THIS PRETTY WELL.

SHOCKER, RIGHT? I GUESS I'M TOO WORRIED ABOUT JASON. WE'VE ONLY BEEN TOGETHER A FEW WEEKS, BUT WE'RE REALLY INTO EACH OTHER, YOU KNOW?

I DON'T HAVE TO TELL YOU. I CAN SEE HOW WORRIED YOU ARE ABOUT PERCY.

PIPER, ABOUT THAT.

PERCY AND I HAVE KNOWN EACH OTHER FOR YEARS.

WE SPENT SUMMERS TOGETHER, WENT ON QUESTS TOGETHER. BUT...

LOOK, I KNOW JASON THINKS HE JUST APPEARED AT OUR SCHOOL TODAY, BUT THAT'S NOT TRUE. I'VE KNOWN HIM FOR FOUR MONTHS.

IT'S THE MIST. IT'S A KIND OF VEIL THAT SEPARATES THE MORTAL WORLD FROM THE MAGIC WORLD. MIST BENDS REALITY, SO MORTALS VIEW THINGS IN A WAY THEY CAN UNDERSTAND.

I'VE SEEN IT LOTS OF TIMES. MIST CAN CHANGE MEMORIES OR EVEN CREATE NEW ONES, SO EVERYONE THINKS THEY REMEMBER STUFF THAT NEVER HAPPENED. MONSTERS USE IT WHEN THEY INFILTRATE A SCHOOL.

YOU KNOW JASON ISN'T A MONSTER! AND MY MEMORIES ARE SO REAL. LIKE WHEN WE WATCHED A METEOR SHOWER ON THE DORM ROOF, AND I FINALLY GOT HIM TO KISS ME.

YOU DON'T JUST MAKE UP STUFF LIKE THAT!

IF YOU KNOW HIM SO WELL, THEN WHERE'S HE FROM? HAVE YOU EVER NOTICED HIS TATTOO BEFORE TODAY?

WHAT'S HIS LAST NAME?

IT'S...I'M SURE I...

OH, GOD. -:sob:-

IT'S OKAY. JASON IS HERE NOW. WHO KNOWS, THIS TIME IT MIGHT WORK OUT WITH YOU GUYS FOR REAL.

MAYBE CHIRON CAN FIGURE OUT WHAT'S GOING ON. BUT IN THE MEANTIME, WE NEED TO GET YOU SETTLED.

FOLLOW ME.

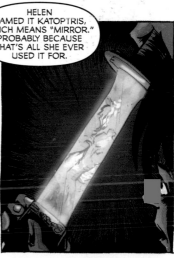

THE CABINS ALL REPRESENT A GREEK GOD. THIS ONE IS HERA'S, RIGHT?

YOU KNOW YOUR MYTHOLOGY.

I DID SOME RESEARCH TO HELP MY DAD WITH A PROJECT LAST YEAR.

WHAT DOES YOUR DAD DO?

HE'S...UH... A CHEROKEE ARTIST. BUT, YOU KNOW, HE GETS HIS INFLUENCES FROM LOTS OF DIFFERENT CULTURES.

ANY CHANCE *HERA* COULD BE MY MOM?

NO WAY. HERA IS THE GODDESS OF MARRIAGE, SO SHE DOESN'T *GET AROUND* LIKE SOME OF THE OTHER GODS DO. SHE ONLY HAS KIDS WITH ZEUS. *ZEUS*, ON THE OTHER HAND...

ANYWAY, THIS CABIN IS JUST HONORARY. *NOBODY* EVER GOES IN THERE.

PIPER! WAIT!

CABIN NINE. THIS IS YOU.

REAL GREEK WARSHIPS ARMED WITH ARROWS AND *EXPLOSIVES*? SCULPTURE CLASS WHERE WE GET TO USE *CHAIN SAWS* AND *BLOWTORCHES*? THIS CAMP IS AWESOME!

WHEN DO I GET A SWORD? I WANT A *SWORD*!

YEAH... WELL, YOU'LL PROBABLY MAKE YOUR OWN.

YOUR DAD *IS* THE GOD OF BLACKSMITHS.

ABOUT THAT: THE RAINBOW PONY DUDE--BUTCH-- HE SAID SOMETHING ABOUT A CURSE. WHAT'D HE MEAN?

OH, YOU KNOW, SINCE CABIN NINE'S LAST COUNSELOR DIED--

DIED?! LIKE, *PAINFULLY*?

WE CAN TALK ABOUT IT INSIDE.

AH! THE OLD LADY... WHAT'S SHE DOING HERE?

WHAT OLD LADY? I DON'T SEE ANYONE.

THAT OLD--

YOU'VE BEEN THROUGH A LOT TODAY. I THINK THE MIST IS STILL PLAYING TRICKS ON YOUR MIND.

NAH, MAN. I'M JUST MESSING WITH YOU. LET'S GO INSIDE.

DUDE.

LOOK AT ALL THIS STUFF. THIS PLACE REMINDS ME OF MY MOM'S MACHINE SHOP. BUT *COOLER*.

YOU THINK YOUR MOM KNOWS WHO YOUR DAD IS? I MEAN, WHO HE *REALLY* IS.

I DON'T KNOW. SHE... DIED WHEN I WAS EIGHT.

WHAT'S THE GOD OF FIRE NEED WITH A *WEED WHACKER*?

YOU'D BE SURPRISED.

WELCOME TO CABIN NINE. I'M JAKE MASON, YOUR HEAD COUNSELOR.

FOR *NOW*.

THIS IS LEO VALDEZ. YOU HAVE A SPARE BUNK FOR HIM?

HE CAN HAVE BECKENDORF'S OLD BED...

...IF HE WANTS IT.

ARE YOU KIDDING? THIS IS THE ROLLS-ROYCE OF BEDS. WHY *WOULDN'T* I WANT IT?

WHOEVER THIS BECKENDORF KID IS, HE'S *NUTS* FOR GIVING IT UP.

HE DIDN'T GIVE IT UP. HE'S THE COUNSELOR I WAS TELLING YOU ABOUT. THE ONE WHO DIED.

DID HE DIE, LIKE, *IN* THE BED?

HE WAS ONE OF THE FIRST CASUALTIES OF THE *TITAN WAR*.

I'M GUESSING BY "TITANS" YOU DON'T MEAN THE FOOTBALL TEAM.

THE TITANS RULED THE WORLD BEFORE THE GODS. THEIR LEADER, KRONOS, TRIED TO MAKE A COMEBACK LAST SUMMER.

A LOT OF DEMIGODS DIED TRYING TO STOP HIM.

BECKENDORF AND PERCY JACKSON BLEW UP A CRUISE SHIP FULL OF MONSTERS. BECKENDORF DIDN'T MAKE IT OUT.

EVER SINCE THEN, THE HEPHAESTUS KIDS HAVE BEEN HAVING PROBLEMS.

EQUIPMENT MALFUNCTIONS, ACCIDENTS...IT'S LIKE OUR WHOLE CABIN HAS BEEN--

CURSED.

WILL, WHY DON'T YOU TAKE LEO DOWNSTAIRS AND SHOW HIM THE FORGES? I'D DO IT MYSELF, BUT...YOU KNOW.

SURE THING, JAKE. YOU GET SOME REST.

HEY, EVERYONE! SAY HELLO TO YOUR NEW *BROTHER*.

CLANK

SKRIIIITCH

JEEZ. YOU WEREN'T KIDDING ABOUT THE ACCIDENTS, WERE YOU?

A MAP OF THE FOREST. WE HAVE A LITTLE BIT OF A...UM... DRAGON PROBLEM.

A *DRAGON* DRAGON?

SORT OF. IT'S LIFE-SIZE, BUT IT'S NOT REAL. I MEAN, IT'S *REAL*, BUT IT'S MADE OF BRONZE. IT'S AN AUTOMATON.

BECKENDORF FOUND IT IN PIECES IN THE WOODS A FEW SUMMERS BACK. HE REBUILT IT, AND IT HELPED PROTECT CAMP DURING THE TITAN WAR.

HE WAS THE ONLY ONE WHO COULD CONTROL IT, THOUGH. AFTER HE DIED, IT WENT HAYWIRE. SMASHING CABINS AND TRYING TO *EAT* THE SATYRS. IT'S KIND OF A NUISANCE.

WE'VE BEEN SETTING TRAPS TO TRY TO CATCH IT, BUT SO FAR, NO LUCK.

IF WE DON'T DESTROY IT SOON, WHO KNOWS WHAT'LL HAPPEN.

DESTROY IT? CAN'T YOU REPAIR IT?

HOW? IT'S GOT RAZOR-SHARP FANGS AND CLAWS AS LONG AS MY ARM. OH, AND IT *BREATHES FIRE*.

OUR DAD IS THE *GOD* OF FIRE.

THAT COMES WITH SOME KIND OF BUILT-IN *IMMUNITY* OR SOMETHING, DOESN'T IT?

WE'RE MOSTLY JUST GOOD WITH OUR HANDS.

BUILDERS, CRAFTSMEN, WEAPONSMITHS... STUFF LIKE THAT.

A CHILD OF HEPHAESTUS *CAN* BE BORN WITH POWER OVER FIRE, BUT THAT HASN'T HAPPENED IN CENTURIES. WHICH IS GOOD, BECAUSE IT USUALLY MEANS SOMETHING *CATASTROPHIC* IS ABOUT TO HAPPEN.

WE DO *NOT* NEED ANY MORE CATASTROPHES.

WE'RE ALL KNOCKING OFF TO GET READY FOR DINNER. YOU WANT TO COME?

I'LL CATCH UP. I WANT TO HANG AROUND A LITTLE LONGER.

SUIT YOURSELF.

WHOOS

SO THE CAMP HAS A DRAGON PROBLEM.

I'LL JUST HAVE TO SEE ABOUT *FIXING* THAT.

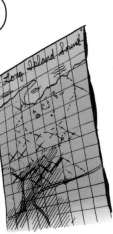

SO HERE WE ARE. CAMP HEADQUARTERS. YOU'LL HAVE TO EXCUSE THE *HIDEOUS* DECOR. IT WAS A PARTING GIFT FROM OUR OLD CAMP DIRECTOR, DIONYSUS.

AS IN DIONYSUS, THE GOD OF WINE?

MM-HMM. HE HAS A THING FOR LEOPARDS, TOO.

OH, CHIRON! THIS IS JASON. HE'S TOTALLY *AWESOME.*

IT'S VERY NICE TO MEET--

YOU...?

YOU SHOULD BE DEAD.

NICE TO MEET YOU, TOO?

TAP TAP

ER, APOLOGIES FOR THE RUDE INTRODUCTION, JASON. PLEASE, HAVE A SEAT.

DREW, YOU MAY RETURN TO YOUR CABIN.

-huff- FINE.

SO, JASON... WOULD YOU MIND TELLING ME WHERE YOU'RE FROM?

DO YOU KNOW WHAT THOSE MARKS ON YOUR FOREARM MEAN, OR THE *PARTICULAR COLOR* OF YOUR SHIRT?

I WISH I COULD. I DON'T REMEMBER MUCH OF ANYTHING BEFORE THIS MORNING.

BUT YOU KNOW WHAT THIS PLACE IS, DON'T YOU? YOU KNOW WHO *I* AM.

YOU'RE CHIRON, FROM THE *MYTHS.* YOU TRAINED HEROES LIKE HERACLES.

AND THIS IS A CAMP FOR THE HALF-BLOOD CHILDREN OF THE OLYMPIAN GODS. THE GODS ARE IN AMERICA NOW BECAUSE THEY FOLLOW THE HEART OF WESTERN CIVILIZATION.

QUITE RIGHT. I COULDN'T HAVE SAID IT BETTER MYSELF.

I TAUGHT YOUR NAMESAKE, YOU KNOW: THE *ORIGINAL* JASON. I'VE SEEN MANY HEROES COME AND GO.

BUT YOU ARE NOT LIKE ANY PUPIL I HAVE EVER HAD.

YOUR PRESENCE HERE COULD BE A *DISASTER.*

YOU SAID I'M SUPPOSED TO BE DEAD... WHAT DOES THAT MEAN?

I'M AFRAID I CAN'T EXPLAIN, MY BOY. I SWORE ON THE *RIVER STYX* THAT I WOULD NEVER TALK ABOUT IT.

BUT YOU ARE HERE IN VIOLATION OF THE SAME OATH. WHO WOULD DO SUCH A THING? WHO--

CHIRON? WHO *WHAT?*

HELLO-O?

GAH!

WHO ARE YOU? WHAT DO YOU WANT?

I AM YOUR *PATRON*, JASON. LONG AGO, YOUR FATHER GAVE ME YOUR LIFE TO PLACATE MY ANGER. I SPARED YOU, AND NOW YOU *BELONG* TO ME.

NOW IT IS TIME TO *REPAY* YOUR DEBT. FIND MY PRISON. *FREE ME*, OR THEIR KING WILL RISE FROM THE EARTH, AND I WILL BE DESTROYED.

YOU HAVE UNTIL SUNSET ON THE *SOLSTICE*. FOUR SHORT DAYS. DO NOT FAIL ME.

--WOULD *DARE* TO BRING YOU HERE?

WHY ARE YOU LOOKING AT ME LIKE THAT, CHILD?

AND WEREN'T YOU JUST SITTING ON THE SOFA...?

SOMETHING WEIRD JUST HAPPENED. IT WAS LIKE TIME *FROZE*. AND THEN--

CHIRON! HELP!

PIPER! WHAT HAPPENED TO HER?

WE WERE IN HERA'S CABIN. SHE HAD SOME SORT OF VISION.

ONE OF RACHEL'S PROPHECIES?

NO. THE SPIRIT OF DELPHI COMES FROM *WITHIN*. THIS WAS LIKE A POWER THAT WAS TRYING TO SPEAK THROUGH ME FROM *FAR AWAY*.

THE VOICE... IT WAS AN OLDER WOMAN. SHE SAID SHE WANTED PIPER TO--

--FREE HER FROM PRISON.

HOW DID YOU--?

AN OLD WOMAN JUST VISITED ME *HERE*. SHE SAID SHE WAS MY PATRON AND THAT I HAD TO FREE HER. SOMETHING ABOUT A KING RISING FROM THE EARTH ON THE SOLSTICE.

YOUR "PATRON"? NOT YOUR GODLY PARENT?

PATRON. SHE WORE A GOATSKIN CLOAK. THAT'S THE SYMBOL OF JUNO, ISN'T IT?

OF COURSE! JUNO IS HERA'S ROMAN ASPECT. THE GOATSKIN CLOAK REPRESENTS THE ROMAN ARMY.

BUT WHY WOULD HERA SEND A MESSAGE TO YOU AND PIPER? YOU JUST GOT HERE.

IF HERA TRULY *IS* IMPRISONED AND IN DANGER OF DESTRUCTION, THIS COULD SHAKE THE FOUNDATIONS OF THE WORLD.

SHE IS THE GLUE THAT HOLDS THE GODS' FAMILY TOGETHER.

IF THE STABILITY OF OLYMPUS WERE TO *UNRAVEL*...

CHIRON, YOU *KNOW* SOMETHING, DON'T YOU? WHAT AREN'T YOU TELLING US?

WHAT COULD BE *STRONG ENOUGH* TO IMPRISON THE QUEEN OF THE GODS? DOES IT HAVE SOMETHING TO DO WITH *PERCY'S* DISAPPEARANCE?

TEND TO THE GIRL. WATCH HER CLOSELY, AND APPRISE ME IF HER CONDITION WORSENS.

CHIRON? YOU'VE *NEVER* KEPT INFORMATION FROM ME. NOT EVEN THE LAST GREAT PROPHECY.

MY DEAR, IN *THIS*, I CANNOT HELP YOU. I AM SORRY.

FINE. IF CHIRON WON'T HELP US, WE'LL HAVE TO FIGURE THIS OUT ON *OUR OWN*.

FIRST ORDER OF BUSINESS: WHERE DID JASON'S MEMORIES GO, AND WHY IS HE SO FOND OF THE GODS' *ROMAN* NAMES?

WHAT DOES THAT MATTER? HERA, JUNO...SAME PERSON, DIFFERENT NAME, RIGHT?

NOT EXACTLY. WE CALL THE GODS BY THEIR GREEK NAMES BECAUSE THAT'S THEIR ORIGINAL FORM, BUT SAYING THEIR ROMAN ASPECTS ARE *EXACTLY* THE SAME--THAT'S NOT TRUE.

THE ROMAN EMPIRE LASTED FOR CENTURIES. THE GODS WERE *ROMAN* ALMOST AS LONG AS THEY WERE *GREEK*. SO OF COURSE THEIR ROMAN ASPECTS ARE STILL A BIG PART OF WHO THEY ARE.

IN ROME, THEY WERE MORE WARLIKE. THEY WERE *HARSHER*, MORE *POWERFUL*. THE GODS OF AN EMPIRE.

IN OTHER WORDS, IF YOU HAD TO MEET THE QUEEN OF THE GODS, YOU'D HOPE SHE WAS MORE IN A *HERA* MOOD THAN A *JUNO* MOOD.

DEFINITELY.

I CAN'T HELP FEELING LIKE THIS IS ALL *MY* FAULT. THAT I DRAGGED PIPER INTO THE MIDDLE OF THIS SOMEHOW. IS SHE GOING TO BE OKAY?

I THINK SO. CHIRON GAVE HER NECTAR OF THE GODS. IT CAN HEAL HALF-BLOODS OF MOST ANYTHING.

IT JUST TAKES TIME.

NO!

TAKE IT EASY, PIPER. IT'S JUST US. YOU'RE SAFE.

WHERE ARE WE?

WE'RE AT THE CAMP OFFICES. ANNABETH AND I BROUGHT YOU HERE WHEN YOU PASSED OUT.

SORRY ABOUT THAT, BY THE WAY. BELIEVE ME, IT WAS *NOT* MY IDEA TO GET POSSESSED.

HERA. SHE *SPOKE* TO ME....

YEAH, THERE'S BEEN *A LOT* OF THAT HAPPENING. WHATEVER IS GOING ON, IT LOOKS LIKE YOU AND I ARE IN IT TOGETHER.

SO IT COULD BE WORSE, RIGHT?

JASON, I...

LATER. ANNABETH SAYS IT'S NOT GOOD TO DRINK NECTAR ON AN EMPTY STOMACH. SOMETHING ABOUT TURNING YOUR BONES TO *ASH*.

LET'S GET SOME DINNER. NOTHING'S MORE RELAXING THAN A GOOD MEAL--

ENOUGH CHITCHAT. HAS THE **SECOND GREAT PROPHECY** BEGUN OR NOT?

I MEAN, COME ON. FIRST PERCY DISAPPEARS, THEN HERA SENDS ANNABETH A VISION ABOUT THE GRAND CANYON, AND SHE COMES BACK WITH **THREE** NEW HALF-BLOODS IN **ONE** DAY. IT'S STARTING, ISN'T IT?

RACHEL?

YES. THE SECOND GREAT PROPHECY **HAS** BEGUN.

FOR THOSE WHO WEREN'T HERE WHEN I SPOKE THE ORACLE'S WORDS LAST AUGUST, THE LINES OF THE PROPHECY GO LIKE THIS:

"SEVEN HALF-BLOODS SHALL ANSWER THE CALL. TO STORM OR FIRE THE WORLD MUST FALL--

"--AN OATH TO KEEP WITH A FINAL BREATH, AND FOES BEAR ARMS TO THE DOORS OF DEATH."

THE SEVEN DEMIGODS, WHOEVER THEY ARE, HAVE NOT BEEN GATHERED YET. I GET THE FEELING SOME ARE HERE TONIGHT, BUT SOME ARE NOT.

WHAT WE DO KNOW IS THE **FIRST PHASE** OF THE PROPHECY HAS BEGUN, AND WE MUST ANSWER THE CALL. HERA, QUEEN OF THE GODS, HAS BEEN CAPTURED.

HERA? HOW...?

DI IMMORTALES.

THE GODS WILL **NOT** BE HAPPY.

KR-KRACK

YAH!

THAT'S NOT... *POSSIBLE.*

A LITTLE *OVERKILL* PERHAPS, BUT I'M AFRAID THE MEANING IS CLEAR.

JASON IS A CHILD OF *ZEUS,* LORD OF THE SKY.

BUT WHAT ABOUT THE *PACT* BETWEEN ZEUS, POSEIDON, AND HADES? THEY SWORE NOT TO HAVE ANY MORE MORTAL KIDS. IF THE OATH HAS BEEN BROKEN *AGAIN*--

WE CAN'T THINK ABOUT THAT NOW. JASON HAS A QUEST TO FULFILL, WHICH MEANS HE'LL NEED HIS *OWN* PROPHECY.

HOO-BOY. I FEEL SOMETHING COMING ON HERE.

-ahem-

CHILD OF LIGHTNING, BEWARE THE EARTH.

THE GIANTS' REVENGE, THE SSSEVEN SHALL BIRTH.

THE FORGE AND DOVE SSSHALL BREAK THE CAGE.

AND DEATH UNLEASSSH THROUGH HERA'S RAGE.

EASY, RACHEL...

IS THIS, LIKE, A REGULAR THING WITH HER?

HAPPENS ALL THE TIME. SHE'LL BE FINE.

THE GIANTS' REVENGE... IT CAN'T BE.

DON'T SPEAK OF IT. IT WILL ONLY SCARE THEM. IF WE ARE TO HAVE ANY HOPE, THEY MUST HAVE *COURAGE*.

NOW, THEN. JASON IS OBVIOUSLY THE CHILD OF LIGHTNING THAT THE PROPHECY SPEAKS OF. THE QUEST IS HIS.

ACCORDING TO TRADITION, HE MAY CHOOSE ANY *TWO* COMPANIONS.

OKAY, NO NEED TO *BEG*. WE BOTH KNOW I'M SUPPOSED TO GO. IT'S *GOTTA* BE, RIGHT? THE FORGE IS THE SYMBOL OF HEPHAESTUS.

BESIDES, THE SMOKE-GIRL OVER THERE SAID YOU SHOULD "BEWARE THE EARTH." I MAY HAVE A WAY TO GET US SOME *AIR* TRANSPORTATION.

THANKS, MAN. IT DOES SEEM ONLY RIGHT YOU COME ALONG. YOU FIND US A RIDE, AND YOU'RE IN.

THAT JUST LEAVES THE DOVE. NOW--

OH, *ABSOLUTELY*. THE DOVE IS APHRODITE. EVERYONE KNOWS THAT. I'M *TOTALLY* YOURS.

WE CAN SIT IN BACK WHILE THE HAMMERHEAD DRIVES.

NO! *I'M* SUPPOSED TO GO! I HAD A VISION OF HERA, *TOO!*

-*pfft*- *SURE* YOU DID, DUMPSTER GIRL. WHAT USE COULD YOU POSSIBLY BE ON A QUEST?

I HAVE *CHARM*. WHAT DO *YOU* HAVE?

-:*gasp!*:-

WHAT'S GOING ON? IS SOMEONE *DOING* SOMETHING TO ME?

HOW DID--?

NO! SHE *CAN'T* BE! SHE'S--

BEAUTIFUL.

PIPER, YOU'RE A *KNOCKOUT.*

I-I DON'T UNDERSTAND. THESE AREN'T *MY* CLOTHES.

IF I WERE A DRAGON, WHERE WOULD I BE...?

SNORT

OH. UM... HEY. *EASY* THERE, BIG FELLA.

I'M HERE TO HELP. THE REST OF CAMP WANTS TO SEND YOU TO THE *SCRAP HEAP*, BUT I THINK I CAN FIX YOU.

WAIT!

FWOOOSH

SNRT?

NOT *EXACTLY* THE WELCOME I WAS HOPING FOR.

BOOM BOOM BOOM

AAAA! STAY BACK! I'M FIREPROOF, NOT *TRAMPLE-PROOF!*

CREAK

IS THAT... ARE YOU SHOWING ME AN ACCESS PANEL?

WHAT'S INSIDE THERE, BOY?

FLIP

NO *WONDER* YOU'VE BEEN ACTING UP. YOUR CIRCUITS ARE FRIED. AND YOUR CONTROL DISK IS A *MESS!*

LET'S SEE WHAT YOUR PAL LEO CAN DO.

I...I *REMEMBER* THIS PLACE.

GRRR

SNARL

LUPA, IS THAT YOU? I REMEMBER YOU, TOO.

AS YOU SHOULD. I FOUND YOU IN THIS PLACE LONG AGO. I PROTECTED YOU, NURTURED YOU. *CHOSE* YOU.

YOU BEGAN YOUR JOURNEY HERE, AND NOW YOU MUST FIND YOUR WAY *BACK.* A NEW QUEST. A NEW START.

RUMBLLLL

RUM BL

HERA!

"YOU'RE SO *LUCKY* TO BE IN CABIN ONE, JASON! IT'S SUCH AN *HONOR!*"

YEAH, RIGHT. DOESN'T ANYONE AROUND HERE KNOW ONE IS THE *LONELIEST* NUMBER?

-*cough*- GUESS IT'S BEEN A WHILE SINCE ANYONE SLEPT HERE.

THAT'S THALIA.

SHE'S THE ONLY OTHER CHILD OF ZEUS--AT LEAST THAT WE KNOW OF. SHE STAYED HERE FOR A LITTLE WHILE, BUT NOW SHE'S ONE OF *ARTEMIS'S HUNTERS*. THEY ROAM THE COUNTRY KILLING MONSTERS.

SOUNDS DANGEROUS.

YEAH, WELL, THEY NEVER AGE, SO IT ISN'T *ALL* BAD.

I DON'T SUPPOSE YOU'D LIKE TO JOIN OUR QUEST? DON'T TELL PIPER AND LEO, BUT I HAVE *ZERO* IDEA WHAT I'M SUPPOSED TO DO.

SORRY, BUT FINDING PERCY IS MY PRIORITY. YOU DON'T NEED ME ANYWAY. SOMETHING TELLS ME THIS ISN'T YOUR FIRST QUEST, WHETHER YOU REMEMBER IT OR NOT.

BESIDES, ALL YOU HAVE TO DO IS FOLLOW THE MONSTERS. YOU WERE ATTACKED BY STORM SPIRITS ON THE SKYWALK, RIGHT? SO I'D START WITH THE NEAREST WIND GOD.

NO PROBLEM. THERE MUST BE A GODS-AND-MONSTERS *PHONE BOOK*, RIGHT?

ACTUALLY, THERE *IS*. BUT YOU DON'T NEED IT. BOREAS, THE NORTH WIND, IS THE CLOSEST TO WHERE WE ARE. HE LIVES IN QUEBEC CITY.

THANKS.

SO, YOU AND THALIA WERE FRIENDS? SOMETHING ABOUT HER... FEELS FAMILIAR. WHAT'S HER LAST NAME?

SHE RAN AWAY FROM HOME WHEN SHE WAS PRETTY YOUNG. SHE AND HER MOM DIDN'T GET ALONG, AND THALIA DIDN'T LIKE TO USE THE FAMILY NAME. BUT I THINK IT WAS "GRACE."

"YOU ARE OUR SAVING *GRACE*, AS ALWAYS."

NNGH!

WHAT'S WRONG?

I-I DON'T KNOW HOW, BUT I *REMEMBER*. ANNABETH, *MY* LAST NAME IS GRACE.

THALIA...

SHE'S MY *SISTER*.

UGH.

SHAKE
RUB

-sigh-

IT'S BACK! IT'S BACK!

IT'S HEADED THIS WAY! EVERYONE GET TO THE ARMORY!

-pfft- COUNT ME OUT.

WILL! DEPLOY THE ARCHERS AT THEIR POSTS!

SOMEBODY WARN THE SATYRS!

LEO?!

LEO? WHERE DID YOU...?

I SAID I'D FIND US SOME AIR TRANSPORTATION. DID I **COME THROUGH** OR WHAT?

YEAH, BUT... HOW DID YOU SURVIVE THE **FIRE BREATH?**

I...UH... GOT LUCKY.

FESTUS IS ACTUALLY REALLY NICE. HE JUST NEEDED LITTLE **TUNE-UP** HE'S AS GOOD AS NEW.

I THINK.

NOW, I SUGGEST YOU CLIMB ABOARD, SO WE CAN GET GOING. ALL THESE WEAPONS ARE MAKING FESTUS NERVOUS.

BUT WE HAVEN'T PLANNED ANYTHING YET. WE CAN'T JUST--

GO. IF A PET DRAGON ISN'T A GOOD OMEN, I DON'T KNOW WHAT IS.

ALL RIGHT. ONLY THREE DAYS UNTIL THE SOLSTICE, SO TIME IS WASTING.

YOU STILL LOOK...

DON'T REMIND ME. THEY SAY APHRODITE'S BLESSING CAN LAST AS LONG AS A **WEEK!**

AT LEAST MY CABINMATES LENT ME SOME BETTER CLOTHES.

EVERYBODY HANG ON!

THERE ARE TONS OF GIANTS IN GREEK MYTHOLOGY, BUT IF IT'S THE ONES I'M THINKING OF, THEY WERE--*ARE*--BAD NEWS.

THERE'S A WHOLE ARMY OF THEM, AND THEY'RE ALMOST IMPOSSIBLE TO KILL. THEY CAN THROW WHOLE *MOUNTAINS* AND STUFF.

THEY ROSE FROM THE EARTH THOUSANDS OF YEARS AGO, AFTER KRONOS LOST THE TITAN WAR.

IF WE'RE TALKING ABOUT THE SAME GIANTS, THEY TRIED TO DESTROY OLYMPUS.

WHEN HE WAS GIVING ME THE TOUR, WILL TOLD ME THERE WAS *ANOTHER* TITAN WAR LAST SUMMER. KRONOS CAME BACK AND TRIED TO OVERTHROW THE GODS.

IF GREEK MYTHOLOGY IS REPEATING ITSELF, THEN THAT MEANS THE GIANTS ARE NEXT.

YOU SAID THESE GIANTS ROSE FROM THE EARTH? THE WOLF I WAS TELLING YOU ABOUT...I DREAMED LAST NIGHT ABOUT A BURNED-OUT HOUSE IN A REDWOOD FOREST.

THE WOLF WAS THERE. THESE TWO HUGE SPIRES ROSE OUT OF THE GROUND. ONE HAD A CAGE WITH HERA INSIDE. THE OTHER WAS FUSED SHUT...BUT I GOT THE FEELING IT HELD SOMETHING *REALLY* BAD.

YOU GUYS KEEP MENTIONING "EARTH" AND "GROUND." I DON'T KNOW IF IT'S IMPORTANT, BUT...I'VE NEVER TOLD ANYONE THIS BEFORE...

THE NIGHT MY MOM DIED...I WAS ONLY EIGHT YEARS OLD. WE WERE AT HER MACHINE SHOP. I WAS VISITED BY THIS WOMAN.

AT LEAST, I *THINK* IT WAS A WOMAN. SHE WAS MADE OF DIRT, AND SHE LOOKED LIKE SHE WAS SLEEPING. I TRIED TO PROTECT MY MOM FROM HER, BUT...

I NEVER SAW THE DIRT-LADY AGAIN AFTER THAT NIGHT.

I NEVER SAW TÍA CALLIDA, MY OLD BABYSITTER, AGAIN EITHER. UNTIL *YESTERDAY*.

I SAW HER AT CAMP. SHE WAS DRESSED IN A BLACK ROBE, AND SHE WAS JUST *STARING* AT ME. THE WEIRD THING WAS, NOBODY ELSE SEEMED TO NOTICE HER.

YESTERDAY? THAT COULD'VE BEEN THE SAME TIME PIPER AND I WERE HAVING OUR VISIONS OF HERA. WHAT IF YOUR BABYSITTER WAS REALLY HERA, QUEEN OF THE GODS?

DID I *ACTUALLY* JUST SAY THAT?

IT MAKES SENSE. THE THREE OF US HAVE DEFINITELY BEEN CHOSEN BY HERA. THE QUESTION IS WHY?

WE'D BETTER FIND OUT. AND FAST.

SO, YOUR DAD'S AN ACTOR?

HE'S TRISTAN MCLEAN. BUT DON'T TELL ANYONE. I DON'T LIKE FOR PEOPLE TO KNOW.

IS HE FAMOUS OR SOMETHING?

I KEEP FORGETTING ABOUT YOUR AMNESIA. HE WAS THE LEAD IN *KING OF SPARTA*. IT ONLY MADE, LIKE, A *BAJILLION* DOLLARS AT THE BOX OFFICE.

COOL. I WONDER IF I'VE SEEN IT....

LATER.

QUEBEC CITY, CANADA.

HEADS UP. WE GOT INCOMING.

NO CLEARANCE!

RESTRICTED AIRSPACE!

WHO'RE YOU, CANADIAN AIR TRAFFIC CONTROL?

THIS IS MY BROTHER, CALAIS. I AM ZETHE. WE ARE THE *BOREADS*.

WE ARE THE GATEKEEPERS. YOU DON'T HAVE A REGISTERED FLIGHT PLAN, SO WE MUST DESTROY YOU.

DESTROY!

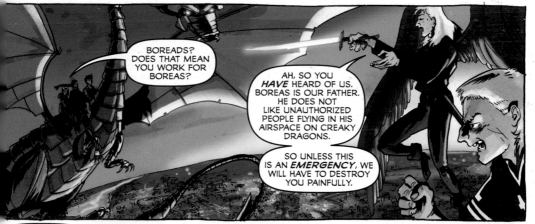

BOREADS? DOES THAT MEAN YOU WORK FOR BOREAS?

AH, SO YOU *HAVE* HEARD OF US. BOREAS IS OUR FATHER. HE DOES NOT LIKE UNAUTHORIZED PEOPLE FLYING IN HIS AIRSPACE ON CREAKY DRAGONS.

SO UNLESS THIS IS AN *EMERGENCY*, WE WILL HAVE TO DESTROY YOU PAINFULLY.

AN EMERGENCY...?

OH, BUT THIS *IS* AN EMERGENCY.

OUR DRAGON IS *MALFUNCTIONING*. IT COULD CRASH *ANY MINUTE*. ONLY YOUR DAD CAN *HELP* US!

WELL, YOU ARE PRETTY.

I MEAN, YOU ARE *RIGHT*. A MALFUNCTIONING DRAGON IS VERY BAD. COME, WE WILL ESCORT YOU TO THE HANGAR.

NO DESTROY?

HOW'D YOU DO THAT?

POWER OF PERSUASION. I GUESS I INHERITED IT FROM MY *MOM*.

FIX THE THERMOSTAT IN HERE, AND I'D *TOTALLY* MOVE IN.

NOT ME. SOMETHING FEELS *WRONG* ABOUT THIS PLACE....

SNIFF SNIFF

FIRE. BAD.

SOMETHING IS *VERY* WRONG.

WHO ARE YOU? A CHILD OF THE *SOUTH WIND*, COME TO SPY ON US?

DESTROY AGAIN!

ME? *NO!*

DO NOT TRY TO TRICK US. WE CAN *SMELL* FIRE. I THOUGHT IT WAS THE DRAGON, BUT IT IS *YOU.*

UM... HELP?

TAKE IT EASY. WE'RE NOT HERE TO FIGHT. LEO IS A SON OF HEPHAESTUS.

PIPER IS A DAUGHTER OF APHRODITE. AND I'M ZEUS'S KID.

ZEUS?

IF YOU ARE A SON OF ZEUS, YOU COULD BE THE ONE WE ARE WAITING FOR.

NO DESTROY AGAIN?

WAITING FOR HIM IN A *GOOD* WAY, AS IN YOU'LL SHOWER HIM WITH FABULOUS PRIZES? OR IN A *BAD* WAY, LIKE HE'S IN TROUBLE?

THAT DEPENDS ON MY FATHER'S WILL.

IT FELL TO AEOLUS TO TRACK THE STORM SPIRITS DOWN AND RETURN THEM TO HIS FORTRESS. THE GODS OFFERED NO HELP, EVEN THOUGH THEY WERE THE CAUSE OF THE SPIRITS' RELEASE.

THEN, LAST SUMMER, KRONOS UNLEASHED TYPHON, AND ONCE AGAIN THE GODS DEFEATED HIM. AND, *ONCE AGAIN*, THE STORM SPIRITS WERE LOOSED. AEOLUS HAS BEEN CHASING THEM EVER SINCE.

WHAT DOES THAT HAVE TO DO WITH HALF-BLOODS? IT SOUNDS LIKE THE *GODS* ARE WHO AEOLUS SHOULD BE MAD AT.

AEOLUS CANNOT *VENT* HIS ANGER ON TH GODS. THEY ARE TOO POWERFUL. SO HE GOES AFTE THEIR CHILDREN INSTEAD.

WITH *ONE* EXCEPTION. AEOLUS SAID A SON OF ZEUS MIGHT SEEK MY AID, AND IF THIS HAPPENED, I SHOULD HEAR YOU OUT.

HE SAID YOU COULD MAKE ALL OF OUR LIVES...INTERESTING. SO SPEAK. THEN I WILL DECIDE WHETHER TO LET YOU GO OR NOT.

MY FATHER GIVES ME SUCH LOVELY PRESENTS, JASON....

"JOIN OUR COURT. WE CAN MAKE TIME *FREEZE*."

Z~Z~ZAP

YOU RECOGNIZE ME BETTER *THIS* WAY, YES? AND YET YOU COME TO ME FROM *CAMP HALF-BLOOD.*

HERA'S GAME IS BOLD. AND DANGEROUS. IF SHE FAILS, THE DEMIGODS WILL TEAR EACH OTHER APART.

AQUILON?

YOU KNOW THIS GUY? WHAT'D HE DO WITH BOREAS?

HE *IS* BOREAS. JUST IN ROMAN FORM.

I DON'T KNOW WHY HE SWITCHED.

YOU MAY HAVE THE AID YOU SEEK. I WILL *ENJOY* SEEING HERA'S GAMBLE PLAY OUT--NO MATTER THE RESULT. GO TO THE WINDY CITY.

CHICAGO?

THERE YOU WILL FIND THE ROGUE STORM SPIRITS. IF YOU CAN DEFEAT THE ONE WHO CONTROLS THEM, THEN CAPTURE THEM AND TAKE THEM TO AEOLUS.

AEOLUS POSSESSES THE KNOWLEDGE OF ALL THE WINDS OF EARTH.

EVERY SECRET FINDS ITS WAY TO HIS FORTRESS EVENTUALLY. HE CAN GUIDE YOU ON YOUR QUEST FOR THE QUEEN.

IF HE *CHOOSES* TO.

WHEN YOU FIND YOURSELF BEFORE AEOLUS--IF YOU DO NOT *DIE* ALONG THE WAY--TELL HIM HIS OLD FRIEND BOREAS SENT YOU.

BUT HEAR ME WELL, DEMIGODS: BEFORE THIS QUEST IS OVER, YOU WILL WISH I HAD LISTENED TO MY DAUGHTER, KHIONE--

--AND KEPT YOU FROZEN HERE. *FOREVER.*

JASON? WHAT'RE YOU... HOW ARE YOU...?
I'M AS SURPRISED AS YOU ARE.
ZEUS IS LORD OF THE SKY. FLYING MUST COME WITH THE TERRITORY. THANKFULLY.
SORRY! YOU TWO ARE HEAVY ENOUGH AS IT IS!
WHAT'S THAT SUPPOSED TO MEAN?!
WELL, FLY THEN!
I'M TRYING! THE BEST I CAN DO IS SLOW US DOWN!
WHAT ABOUT FESTUS? WE CAN'T LET HIM CRASH!
MONOCLE MOTORS
BRACE FOR IMPACT!

I CAN'T PUT ANY WEIGHT ON IT.

OKAY, JUST LIE STILL.

LEO, DO YOU HAVE ANY FIRST AID SUPPLIES?

SURE. LET'S SEE...DUCT TAPE AND BANDAGES.

PRESTO! MAGIC TOOL BELT.

I HAVEN'T FIGURED IT OUT COMPLETELY, BUT I CAN SUMMON JUST ABOUT ANY REGULAR TOOL FROM THE POCKETS. PLUS SOME OTHER HELPFUL STUFF. PRETTY COOL, HUH?

WHERE'D YOU GET THAT?

OH, UH, I FOUND IT IN THE WOODS. THE NIGHT I FIXED FESTUS.

SPEAKING OF FESTUS... WHAT THE HECK HAPPENED TO HIM?

NO IDEA. ONE MINUTE WE WERE CRUISING ALONG, AND THE NEXT HE JUST JERKED TO THE SIDE, LIKE HE FLEW INTO AN INVISIBLE WALL OR SOMETHING.

RRRRIP

IT'S ALL MY FAULT.

YOU WERE SLEEPING. HOW COULD IT BE YOUR FAULT?

YEAH, YOU'RE JUST SHAKEN UP. TRY TO REST.

YOU GOT THIS? I THINK I SAW WHERE FESTUS CRASHED DOWN. I WANT TO SEE IF HE'S SALVAGEABLE.

GO AHEAD. WE'LL WAIT HERE FOR YOU.

DRINK THIS NECTAR. IT'LL HELP YOUR ANKLE HEAL. GO EASY ON IT, THOUGH.

I DON'T KNOW HOW TO SAY THIS...BUT YOU LOOK LIKE *YOU* AGAIN. I GUESS APHRODITE'S BLESSING FINALLY WENT AWAY.

REALLY? *ABOUT TIME!*

JUST MY LUCK. I FINALLY WANT TO SEE MY REFLECTION, AND THERE'S NO MIRROR IN SIGHT.

YOU LOOK *GREAT.* TRUST ME.

IT FEELS BETTER ALREADY. WHERE'D YOU LEARN FIRST AID?

SAME ANSWER AS ALWAYS. I DON'T KNOW.

BUT YOU'RE STARTING TO HAVE SOME MEMORIES, AREN'T YOU? LIKE THAT DREAM ABOUT THE WOLF.

IT'S FUZZY. EVER FORGOTTEN A WORD OR A NAME, AND YOU KNOW IT SHOULD BE ON THE TIP OF YOUR TONGUE? IT'S LIKE THAT, ONLY WITH MY *WHOLE LIFE*.

I DID REMEMBER *ONE THING*, THOUGH. I HAVE A SISTER. HER NAME IS THALIA. SHE USED TO BE AT CAMP HALF-BLOOD, BUT SHE HUNTS MONSTERS WITH ARTEMIS NOW.

I GET THE FEELING THAT MEMORY WAS LEFT IN MY HEAD FOR A REASON. LIKE I'M *SUPPOSED* TO FIND HER BECAUSE SHE'S CONNECTED TO THIS QUEST. BUT I DON'T KNOW HOW.

I'M NOT SURE I *WANT* TO KNOW....

ABOUT THIS QUEST. JASON...THERE'S SOMETHING I NEED TO TELL YOU--

SHH! DO YOU HEAR THAT?

IT SOUNDS LIKE FOOTSTEPS.

LEO? IS THAT YOU?

I DON'T LIKE THIS. HE COULD BE IN TROUBLE.

WHAT SHOULD WE DO? I DON'T THINK I CAN WALK YET.

I'LL CHECK IT OUT. YOU STAY OUT OF SIGHT.

IT HAS BEEN TOO LONG, LEO VALDEZ.

YOU! Y-YOU'RE...THE DIRT-LADY.

YOU KILLED MY MOM!

AH, BUT I AM YOUR MOTHER, TOO. THE FIRST MOTHER. DO NOT OPPOSE ME. LET MY SON PORPHYRION RISE AND BECOME KING.

YOU ARE THE MOST IMPORTANT OF THE SEVEN--LIKE THE CONTROL DISK IN THE DRAGON'S BRAIN. WITHOUT YOU, THE POWERS OF THE OTHERS MEAN NOTHING. THEY WILL NOT STOP ME. AND I WILL FULLY WAKE.

LADY, YOU GOT SOME NERVE ASKING ME FOR FAVORS. YOU RUINED MY LIFE!

NO. I MADE YOU WHO YOU ARE. WALK AWAY FROM YOUR QUEST, AND YOU WILL TREAD EASILY ON THE EARTH FOR THE REST OF YOUR DAYS. WALK AWAY NOW.

WHY? ARE JASON AND PIPER IN TROUBLE? WHAT DID YOU DO?

THE EARTH HAS MANY HORRORS TO YIELD UP. MONSTERS ARE FREE FROM THEIR PRISON IN TARTARUS, AND SOULS ARE NO LONGER CONFINED TO HADES.

WALK AWAY.

THANKS TO YOU, MY FRIENDS ARE ALL I'VE GOT--

--AND I PLAN ON STICKING WITH THEM!

LEO, THAT WAS *AMAZING!* HOW'D YOU *DO* THAT?

UNIVERSAL REMOTE. THIS TOOL BELT IS THE GIFT THAT KEEPS ON GIVING.

NOT *THAT!* THE FIRE-LASER BEAM THING.

OH, YEAH. I CAN SORT OF MAKE MY OWN FIRE.

I SHOULD'VE TOLD YOU GUYS EARLIER.

SORRY.

SORRY? SORRY FOR *WHAT?* YOU TOTALLY SAVED OUR LIVES!

GLAD TO HELP.

GUYS, LOOK.

TARTARUS? I REMEMBER READING ABOUT THAT PLACE. IT'S WHERE THE GODS *LOCK UP* THE MONSTERS THAT POSE A THREAT TO OLYMPUS.

WHAT ABOUT IT?

THE CYCLOPES. THEY'RE *RE-FORMING.* THEY AREN'T SUPPOSED TO DO THAT. ONCE YOU KILL THEM, THEY'RE SUPPOSED TO STAY DEAD FOR AWHILE.

I DON'T KNOW HOW I KNOW THAT, BUT I DO.

"MONSTERS ARE FREE FROM THEIR PRISON IN TARTARUS, AND SOULS ARE NO LONGER CONFINED TO HADES."

I'LL TELL YOU LATER.

RIGHT NOW, I NEED TO FINISH FIXING FESTUS AND GET US OUT OF HERE.

GO ON, FESTUS. YOU CAN'T HANG AROUND HERE, YOU'LL GET TICKETED FOR LOITERING.

WHO'S THE *LUCKY DUCK* THAT GOES FIRST INTO THE SEWER FULL OF STORM SPIRITS?

I'LL GO. BUT YOU GUYS BETTER BE RIGHT BEHIND ME.

I BLOW THIS WHISTLE, THOUGH, YOU COME SAVE THE DAY. GOT IT?

SNRT

WHICH WAY?

THERE'S A DRAFT MOVING SOUTH. SO LET'S GO THE WAY THE WIND BLOWS.

WISH I'D THOUGHT TO PACK A FLASHLIGHT....

YEAH. THAT'LL WORK.

ABOUT THE WHOLE FIRE THING... WHY **DIDN'T** YOU TELL US?

IT'S BEEN A WHILE SINCE I HAD FRIENDS, YOU KNOW? I DIDN'T WANT YOU GUYS TO THINK I WAS A **FREAK**.

I HAVE **LIGHTNING** AND **WIND** POWERS. PIPER CAN **CHARMSPEAK** PEOPLE INTO GIVING HER STUFF. YOU'RE NO MORE A FREAK THAN WE ARE.

YEAH, WELL, THE HEPHAESTUS CABIN DOESN'T SEE FIRE POWERS AS A GOOD THING. NYSSA TOLD ME THEY'RE SUPER RARE. AND WHENEVER A DEMIGOD LIKE ME COMES ALONG, BAD THINGS HAPPEN. **REALLY** BAD.

MAYBE IT'S THE OTHER WAY AROUND. MAYBE PEOPLE WITH SPECIAL GIFTS SHOW UP WHEN BAD THINGS ARE HAPPENING BECAUSE THAT'S WHEN THEY'RE NEEDED MOST.

MAYBE. BUT I'M TELLING YOU... IT ISN'T ALWAYS A GIFT.

THE NIGHT MY MOM DIED. THE DIRT-LADY WAS THERE.... I TRIED TO STOP HER FROM HURTING MY MOM, BUT I ENDED UP BURNING THE WHOLE MACHINE SHOP TO THE GROUND. THE FIRE JUST...CAME OUT OF ME.

IT WASN'T YOUR FAULT. YOU WERE JUST A LITTLE KID. WHOEVER THAT WOMAN WAS, SHE WAS TRYING TO RUIN YOUR CONFIDENCE. SHE STILL IS.

DON'T YOU SEE? SHE'S **AFRAID** OF YOU.

SHE **SHOULD** BE. BECAUSE I'LL--

NO. **WE** WILL. FRIENDS STICK TOGETHER.

THANKS, MAN.

ENOUGH HEART-TO-HEART. I'M GETTING ALL MISTY.

LET'S FIND OUT WHAT DYLAN AND THE OTHER STORM SPIRITS ARE DOING DOWN HERE.

WHERE DO YOU THINK THESE DOORS LEAD?

DIRECTORY

ONLY ONE WAY TO FIND OUT.

LOOKS LIKE A DEPARTMENT STORE DIRECTORY. BUT WHAT KIND OF DEPARTMENT STORE SELLS *WEAPONRY*, *POTIONS*, AND *POISONS*?

LOOK AT ALL THIS STUFF. THIS PLACE MUST BE *PACKED* ON BLACK FRIDAY.

WE FOUND THE STORM SPIRITS. AND THAT'S NOT *ALL*. LOOK.

COACH HEDGE! WE'VE GOT TO GET DOWN THERE!

MAY I HELP YOU FIND SOMETHING?

UM, IS THIS YOUR STORE?

I FOUND IT ABANDONED-- SO MANY STORES ARE THESE DAYS--AND I DECIDED IT WOULD BE THE *PERFECT* PLACE TO SET UP SHOP.

I LOVE OFFERING *QUALITY* GOODS AT A REASONABLE PRICE.

HOW MUCH FOR THE SATYR WITH THE SPORTS FETISH?

I'D BE *DELIGHTED* TO DISCUSS MY INVENTORY.

BUT FIRST, INTRODUCTIONS. I AM THE PRINCESS OF COLCHIS. MY FRIENDS CALL ME YOUR HIGHNESS.

AND YOU ARE...?

MY NAME IS JASON. MY FRIENDS ARE--

JASON, YOU SAY? WHAT AN *INTERESTING* NAME.

THERE ARE *SO MANY* THINGS I WOULD LIKE TO SHOW YOU, JASON. PLEASE, COME.

LET'S GO *SHOPPING*.

SO, WHERE IS COLCHIS, ANYWAY?

WHERE *WAS* COLCHIS.

MY FATHER RULED THE FAR SHORES OF THE BLACK SEA, AS FAR TO THE EAST AS A GREEK SHIP COULD SAIL IN THOSE DAYS.

BUT COLCHIS IS NO MORE. IT WAS LOST EONS AGO.

EONS? HOW OLD ARE YOU?

tsk. A LADY NEVER TELLS HER AGE...OR ASKS IT OF ANOTHER. LET'S JUST SAY THE *IMMIGRATION PROCESS* TO YOUR COUNTRY TOOK QUITE A WHILE.

MY PATRON FINALLY BROUGHT ME THROUGH. SHE MADE THIS DEPARTMENT STORE POSSIBLE.

SHE DOESN'T BRING JUST ANYONE THROUGH, MIND YOU. ONLY THOSE WHO POSSESS SPECIAL *TALENTS*. LIKE ME.

ALL SHE ASKED WAS THAT THE ENTRANCE TO THE STORE BE UNDERGROUND, SO SHE COULD MONITOR MY CLIENTELE. AND SHE REQUESTS A *FAVOR* NOW AND THEN.

BEST *BARGAIN* I'VE MADE IN CENTURIES.

I READ ABOUT YOU...

GUYS, SHE'S EVIL. *SUPER* EVIL. SHE BETRAYED HER FAMILY. I'M PRETTY SURE SHE MURDERED HER OWN BROTHER.

LIES!

I HAVE BEEN CALLED VILLAIN, TRAITOR, EVEN MURDERER. BUT I AM A *VICTIM*. I FELL IN LOVE WITH A HALF-BLOOD WHO MADE PROMISES. WE HAD A BARGAIN!

BUT HE WENT BACK ON HIS WORD. HE TOOK WHAT HE NEEDED AND *ABANDONED* ME.

YOU, ABOVE ALL OTHERS, SHOULD KNOW THIS. YOU WERE *NAMED* AFTER HIM.

JASON? YOU'RE TALKING ABOUT *THE* JASON?

THAT WAS THREE THOUSAND YEARS AGO.

WHY AREN'T YOU DEAD?

I WAS. BUT I HAVE BEEN MADE *FLESH* AND *BLOOD* AGAIN. DEATH NO LONGER HOLDS ME, YOUNG HERO.

MY PATRON KNOWS THAT MONSTERS ARE NOT HER GREATEST SERVANTS. I AM *MORTAL*. I LEARN FROM MY MISTAKES, AND NOW I HAVE RETURNED TO THE LIVING TO AID MY PATRON'S CAUSE. I WILL NOT BE *CHEATED* AGAIN!

I HOPE YOU TAKE PAYMENT IN *HAMMERS*!

BAMF

HAVE FUN PLAYING WITH MY PET *SUN DRAGONS*. GIFTS FROM MY GRANDFATHER, HELIOS.

NOW THEY WILL BE YOUR *DESTRUCTION*.

TA-TA!

YOU AREN'T GETTING AWAY THAT EASILY!

AGH!

SNAP!

BONK

WE NEED BACKUP!

FWEET!
FWEE-
EET!

YOU CAN THANK COACH HEDGE FOR THAT ONE.

HE MADE US PLAY *ULTIMATE FRISBEE* FOR A MONTH.

KRANG

CORRECTION, *WITCH*. THE CONCOCTION IS GOING TO CONSUME EVERYTHING--

--AND DESTROY *YOU*.

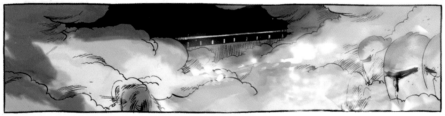

NO!

HRUMPH. HE *EXCELS* AT THAT, BOY. BUT THIS TIME, I SUPPOSE IT IS THE TITAN WAR THAT UPSET HIM. WE GODS WERE...WELL, EMBARRASSED. THERE'S NO OTHER WAY TO SAY IT.

WE ONLY WON BECAUSE THE DEMIGODS OF--

--ER, BECAUSE *OUR CHILDREN* FOUGHT OUR BATTLES FOR US, SMARTER THAN WE DID. IF WE'D STUCK WITH ZEUS'S PLAN, THE WAR WOULD'VE BEEN LOST.

AT FIRST WE WERE GRATEFUL...BUT AS TIME PASSED, THOSE FEELINGS BECAME BITTER. WE'RE *GODS*, AFTER ALL. WE NEED TO BE LOOKED UP TO, HELD IN AWE AND ADMIRATION.

AND THEN WE HEARD OF EVIL THINGS STIRRING UNDER THE EARTH. GIANTS RISING, MONSTERS REFORMING. THE *DEAD* LIVING AGAIN.

ZEUS DECIDED IT WAS TIME TO GET BACK TO TRADITIONAL VALUES. GODS ARE TO BE RESPECTED. OUR CHILDREN ARE TO BE *SEEN* AND NOT *VISITED*.

HE THINKS WE GODS CAN LULL THE EARTH BACK TO SLEEP. NONE OF US REALLY BELIEVES THAT. BUT WE'RE IN NO CONDITION TO FIGHT ANOTHER WAR.

HERA SAID GODS AND DEMIGODS HAVE TO FIGHT TOGETHER.

MY MOTHER PLAYS A DANGEROUS GAME. BUT SHE'S RIGHT ABOUT ONE THING: YOU DEMIGODS HAVE TO UNITE. THAT'S THE ONLY WAY TO DEFEAT WHAT'S COMING.

YOU'RE A BIG PART OF THAT, LEO.

BLAST! ZEUS IS DETECTING AN ILLEGAL DREAM. I CAN'T TALK MUCH LONGER.

FIRE IS A GIFT CRACKLE NOT A CURSE. I DON'T GRANT THAT POWER TO JUST ANYONE.

YOU HAVE A ROLE TO PLAY. YOUR FRIENDS WILL KRSHHH NEVER DEFEAT THE GIANTS WITHOUT YOU. MUCH LESS THE MISTRESS THEY SERVE.

BE WARNED. CRACKLE YOU WILL LOSE SOME FRIENDS AND VALUABLE TOOLS.

EVEN THE BEST MACHINES DON'T LAST FOREVER. BUT EVERYTHING KRSHHH CAN BE REUSED.

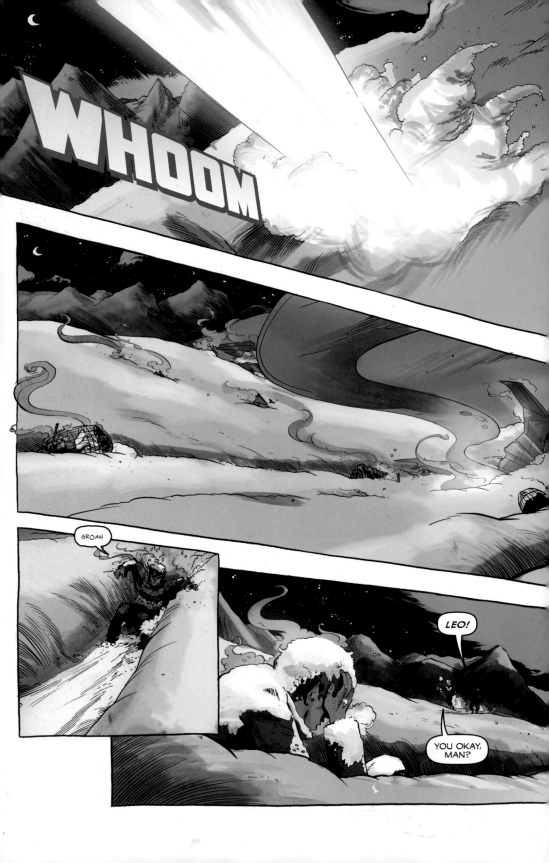

NO...

FESTUS...

YOU WERE THE BEST THING I EVER FIXED.

I'M SORRY, LEO. HE WAS A GREAT DRAGON.

DAD, I'VE NEVER ASKED YOU FOR ANYTHING.

PLEASE, TAKE FESTUS HOME.

UNTIL I CAN FIND A WAY TO REUSE HIM.

THANKS, DAD.

HE *ANSWERED* YOU?

I HAD A DREAM ABOUT HIM. HE ISN'T MUCH OF A LOOKER, BUT I GUESS HE ISN'T SO BAD.

LET'S GATHER THE CAGES AND SALVAGE WHAT SUPPLIES WE CAN. MAYBE THERE'S SOME SHELTER NEARBY.

I'M READY TO GET BACK IN THE GAME, CUPCAKES!

SOMEBODY RECAP THE FIRST HALF FOR ME.

-sigh- IT'LL TAKE A WHILE. WHY DON'T WE SIT DOWN.

AND SO...

--ONLY HAD ONE LEAD ON HOW TO FIND HERA, SO WE WENT TO SEE BOREAS AND ASK HIM ABOUT THE STORM SPIRITS THAT ATTACKED US--

THEN...

--A CYCLOPES FAMILY IN DETROIT. THEY TRIED TO COOK JASON AND PIPER FOR SUPPER--

DON'T FORGET...

--A DEPARTMENT STORE FULL OF ALL KINDS OF WEIRD STUFF. SHE TRIED TO FEED US TO HER PET DRAGONS, BUT I KNOCKED HER INTO A POTIONS DISPLAY--

FINALLY.

--AND FOLLOWED THE MAGIC WIND CURRENT HERE.

WHEREVER HERE IS.

WE'RE ON PIKES PEAK. EVERYONE KNOWS IT'S AEOLUS'S FAVORITE SPOT TO DOCK HIS FLOATING PALACE.

IF BOREAS SAID YOU SHOULD RETURN THE STORM SPIRITS TO THE WIND GOD, THEN YOU CAME TO THE RIGHT PLACE.

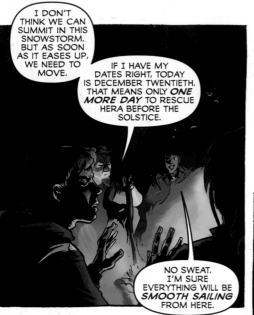

I DON'T THINK WE CAN SUMMIT IN THIS SNOWSTORM. BUT AS SOON AS IT EASES UP, WE NEED TO MOVE.

IF I HAVE MY DATES RIGHT, TODAY IS DECEMBER TWENTIETH. THAT MEANS ONLY *ONE MORE DAY* TO RESCUE HERA BEFORE THE SOLSTICE.

NO SWEAT. I'M SURE EVERYTHING WILL BE *SMOOTH SAILING* FROM HERE.

NIBBLE NIBBLE

~sigh~

GUYS, THERE'S SOMETHING I HAVE TO TELL YOU....

PIPER? WHAT'S WRONG?

OUR FIRST NIGHT AT CAMP, AFTER HERA SPOKE TO ME AND I PASSED OUT...I HAD A DREAM.

A GIANT-- ENCELADUS, HE SAID HIS NAME WAS-- SHOWED ME THAT MY DAD HAD BEEN KIDNAPPED.

HE SAID IF I DIDN'T DO WHAT HE TOLD ME, MY DAD WOULD BE KILLED.

ENCELADUS SAID THERE WOULD BE A *QUEST*, AND THAT I HAD TO GO. HE TOLD ME THE ONLY WAY TO SAVE MY DAD WAS TO MAKE SURE THE QUEST FAILED.

I DIDN'T KNOW THE QUEST WAS GOING TO BE THE THREE OF US. I SWEAR.

THEN I HAD ANOTHER DREAM RIGHT BEFORE FESTUS CRASHED THE FIRST TIME. ENCELADUS TOLD ME TO LEAD YOU GUYS TO A MOUNTAIN IN THE BAY AREA. I DON'T KNOW WHICH ONE EXACTLY,

I'M SUPPOSED TO HAVE YOU THERE BY NOON ON THE SOLSTICE. HE'S GOING TO KILL YOU, AND THEN DAD AND I CAN GO FREE.

PIPER...I'M SO SORRY.

NO KIDDING. YOU'VE BEEN CARRYING THAT AROUND ALL THIS TIME? PIPER, WE CAN HELP YOU.

DON'T YOU UNDERSTAND? I WAS ORDERED TO *KILL* YOU! AND NOW THAT I'VE CONFESSED, MY DAD IS GOING TO *DIE*.

~*humph*~ I DON'T THINK SO. THE GIANT STILL HASN'T GOTTEN WHAT HE WANTS, SO HE'LL KEEP YOUR DAD ALIVE FOR LEVERAGE.

MAYBE JUST EAT ONE OF HIS *ARMS* OR--

COACH!

RIGHT. SORRY.

THERE'S NO WAY HE'D HONOR THE EXCHANGE ANYWAY. IT'S OBVIOUS YOU'RE ONE OF THE SEVEN FROM THE GREAT PROPHECY.

EVEN IF YOU'D DELIVERED JASON AND LEO AS HE COMMANDED, HE WOULD'VE JUST KILLED ALL THREE OF YOU.

AND, OF COURSE, YOUR OLD MAN, TOO.

ONLY THING WE DO KNOW IS, IF HE WANTED YOU TO GO TO THE MOUNTAIN, THEN HERA *DEFINITELY* ISN'T THERE.

HE WOULDN'T LEAD YOU TO HER.

SO WE HAVE NO CHOICE. WE HAVE TO FIND HERA AND SAVE HER, SO PORPHYRION DOESN'T GET UNLEASHED.

MY DAD IS GOING TO DIE....

NOT SO FAST. WE JUST HAVE TO FIGURE OUT A PLAN, IS ALL.

ANY IDEA WHICH MOUNTAIN IN THE BAY AREA?

I'LL KNOW IT IF I SEE IT.

I HOPE IT ISN'T MOUNT TAM. THAT'S THE MODERN LOCATION OF MOUNT OTHRYS, THE FORTRESS OF THE TITANS. IT WAS DESTROYED IN THE TITAN WAR LAST SUMMER.

BAD MOJO THERE.

NO... THAT'S NOT RIGHT.

WHAT DO YOU MEAN? DO YOU REMEMBER THE MOUNTAIN?

HOWOO--

OOOOOO

SOMETHING'S COMING.

NOW WE'RE TALKING!

SO IT'S TRUE. A CHILD OF APHRODITE, A CHILD OF HEPHAESTUS, A SATYR, AND A CHILD OF ROME--OF JUPITER, NO LESS--ALL TOGETHER AND NOT KILLING EACH OTHER.

HOW INTERESTING.

GRRRR SNARL

THANK ARTEMIS! IT *IS* YOU!

WHY DON'T *I* GET TO HAVE A LONG-LOST SISTER WHO MOONLIGHTS AS A WEREWOLF HUNTER?

BUT...SHE TOLD ME YOU WERE DEAD.

WHO TOLD YOU THAT?

DO YOU KNOW WHERE I'VE BEEN ALL THESE YEARS?

I DON'T HAVE MUCH TIME. IF I STAY TOO LONG, I WON'T BE ABLE TO CATCH UP WITH THE REST OF THE HUNTERS.

WE SHOULD TALK, LITTLE BROTHER. IN *PRIVATE*.

WOULD YOU GUYS MIND WAITING OUTSIDE? I'LL BE ALL RIGHT.

NO PROBLEM. THERE'S ONLY A *BLIZZARD* GOING ON OUT THERE.

"SHE KNEW DAD WAS ZEUS, AND SHE COULDN'T ACCEPT IT WHEN HE LEFT. HOW DO YOU FIND A BOYFRIEND TO REPLACE THE *KING* OF THE *GODS*?"

"I THINK SHE DID ALL THOSE DUMB THINGS TO GET HIS ATTENTION. IT MUST'VE WORKED, BECAUSE WHEN I WAS ABOUT SEVEN, DAD CAME BACK."

"THAT WAS THE YEAR YOU WERE BORN. ZEUS STUCK AROUND FOR A WHILE, BUT OF COURSE IT DIDN'T LAST.

"WHEN HE LEFT THE SECOND TIME MOM LOST IT FOR GOOD."

IT DIDN'T HELP THAT THE *MONSTERS* HAD STARTED ATTACKING ME. MOM BLAMED HERA, SAYING SHE WAS JEALOUS BECAUSE ZEUS HAD FATHERED NOT ONE, BUT *TWO* CHILDREN WITH HER.

SHE FIGURED IT WAS ONLY A MATTER OF TIME BEFORE THE MONSTERS STARTED COMING AFTER YOU, TOO.

"WHEN YOU WERE ABOUT TWO, MOM TOOK US ON A FAMILY VACATION. WE WENT TO A PARK IN THE CALIFORNIA WINE COUNTRY. I REMEMBER THINKING IT WAS WEIRD, BECAUSE SHE NEVER TOOK US ANYWHERE.

"I REMEMBER HOLDING YOUR HAND AS WE WALKED TOWARD THIS BIG BUILDING--

"MOM TOLD ME TO GO BACK TO THE CAR TO GET THE PICNIC BASKET.

"I DIDN'T WANT TO LEAVE YOU ALONE WITH HER...."

"I WAS ONLY GONE A FEW MINUTES.

"WHEN I CAME BACK, SHE WAS CRYING ON THE GROUND. SHE SAID YOU WERE GONE.

"HERA HAD CLAIMED YOU, AND YOU WERE AS GOOD AS DEAD."

I LOOKED ALL OVER FOR YOU, BUT I NEVER SAW YOU AGAIN. NOT LONG AFTER THAT DAY, I RAN AWAY. I COULDN'T FORGIVE MOM. NOT FOR SOMETHING LIKE THAT. NOT EVEN AFTER SHE DIED.

I'VE NEVER TOLD ANYONE ABOUT YOU. IT HURT TOO MUCH TO TALK ABOUT. I JUST TRIED TO FORGET.

CHIRON KNEW. WHEN HE SAW ME FOR THE FIRST TIME, HE TOLD ME I SHOULD BE DEAD.

BUT... HOW COULD *HE* KNOW?

THALIA, IS THERE ANOTHER PLACE FOR DEMIGODS? BESIDES CAMP HALF-BLOOD, I MEAN.

THERE ARE THESE WEIRD THINGS ABOUT ME.

FOR SOME REASON I THINK OF THE GODS BY THEIR ROMAN NAMES. AND I HAVE THIS TATTOO.

I HAVEN'T HEARD OF ANYTHING. UNLESS...

NO, THAT COULDN'T BE TRUE.

UNLESS WHAT?

NOTHING. I'LL HAVE TO CONSULT WITH ARTEMIS. LUCKILY, SHE ISN'T OBEYING ZEUS'S ORDER TO BREAK OFF CONTACT WITH MORTALS.

I'M SORRY, BUT I HAVE TO GO. I ASSUME YOU'RE HERE TO RETURN THOSE STORM SPIRITS TO AEOLUS? I CAN ESCORT YOU TO HIS PALACE, BUT THEN I MUST RETURN TO THE HUNTERS.

OH, RIGHT. I DON'T SUPPOSE YOU HAVE A WAY FOR US TO LUG THAT CAGE UP THE MOUNTAIN?

ACTUALLY, I HAVE JUST THE THING.

"LET'S GO SEE THE GOD OF THE WINDS."

THIS PLACE DOESN'T LOOK SO SCARY.

YOU THREE GO AHEAD. I'M GOING TO SNACK--

ER, I MEAN *"SCOUT"* OUT THE PASTURE.

WOO-HOO!

THIS PLACE IS *HUGE*. HOW ARE WE SUPPOSED TO FIND AEOLUS?

WELCOME TO THE HEADQUARTERS OF *OLYMPUS WEATHER CHANNEL!* I'M MELLIE, LORD AEOLUS'S PERSONAL ASSISTANT.

ARE YOU FROM LORD ZEUS? WE'VE BEEN EXPECTING YOU.

I'M JASON. I'M THE SON OF ZEUS.

EXCELLENT! FOLLOW ME, PLEASE.

WE'RE OUT OF PRIME TIME RIGHT NOW, SO THAT'S CONVENIENT.

I MAY BE ABLE TO FIT YOU IN BEFORE AEOLUS GOES LIVE FOR HIS 11:12 UPDATE.

TAP TAP

MAIN STUDIO

SO SORRY!

I FORGET NOT EVERYONE CAN PASS THROUGH *CLOSED* DOORS.

RIGHT THIS WAY.

I'M GLAD I DIDN'T IMPOSE, EVEN THOUGH I DON'T REMEMBER BEING HERE.

ANYWAY, I BROUGHT YOU THESE ROGUE STORM SPIRITS. BOREAS SENT US TO CAPTURE THEM FOR YOU. WE HOPE YOU'LL ACCEPT THEM AND STOP...UM...ORDERING DEMIGODS TO BE KILLED.

DEMIGODS BE KILLED? DID I ORDER THAT, MELLIE?

TAKE THESE TO CELL BLOCK FOURTEEN E.

YES, SIR. I HAVE THE MEMO RIGHT HERE:

"STORM SPIRITS RELEASED BY THE DEATH OF TYPHON. ALL DEMIGODS ARE TO BE HELD RESPONSIBLE. KILL ON SIGHT."

OH, PISH! I WAS JUST GRUMPY. HAVE THAT ORDER RESCINDED, MELLIE.

CONSIDER IT DONE, SIR.

YOU KNOW, I REMEMBER GIVING THAT ORDER. IT WAS ALMOST AS THOUGH I HEARD A VOICE TELLING ME TO DO IT.

BROADCASTING IN THREE...TWO...

THERE'S MY CUE!

"WE'RE LIVE!"

HELLO-O, OLYMPUS!

AEOLUS, MASTER OF THE WINDS, HERE WITH YOUR WEATHER EVERY TWELVE.

SO, YOU BROUGHT ME SOME ROGUE STORM SPIRITS. I SUPPOSE...THANKS!

DID YOU WANT ANYTHING ELSE? DEMIGODS ALWAYS DO.

ACTUALLY, WE'RE ON A QUEST, AND WE NEED YOUR HELP.

WE JUST WANT INFORMATION. WE HEAR YOU KNOW EVERYTHING.

WELL, THAT'S TRUE, OF COURSE. FOR INSTANCE, I KNOW THAT JUNO'S *HAREBRAINED SCHEME* IS LIKELY TO END IN BLOODSHED.

AS FOR YOU, PIPER MCLEAN, I KNOW YOUR FATHER IS IN SERIOUS TROUBLE.

ALL THINGS LOST IN THE WIND EVENTUALLY COME TO ME.

THIS... THIS IS THE PHOTO DAD KEEPS IN HIS WALLET...

DO YOU KNOW WHERE IT CAME FROM?

NATURALLY. MY WINDS CARRIED IT HERE WHEN IT FELL FROM HIS POCKET.

CAN YOU ALSO TELL US WHERE HERA IS BEING HELD CAPTIVE?

GOOD HEAVENS, NO. THERE'S A VEIL OF MAGIC HIDING HER LOCATION. VERY STRONG.

VERY WELL. YOU CAN FIND ENCELADUS AT MOUNT DIABLO.

I REMEMBER THAT PLACE! DAD TOOK ME THERE. IT'S JUST EAST OF SAN FRANCISCO.

BUT ENCELADUS KNOWS. TELL US WHERE TO FIND HIM.

HMM? WHAT'S THAT? I SEE...

ZEUS, APHRODITE, AND HEPHAESTUS *ALL* IN AGREEMENT? THAT *IS* RARE.

WHAT'S THAT?

B-BUT SHE HASN'T SPOKEN TO ME IN CENTURIES. I CAN'T--

YES, YES I UNDERSTAND.

~*ahem*~ APOLOGIES, BUT THERE'S BEEN A *SLIGHT* CHANGE OF PLANS. YOU ALL HAVE TO DIE.

BUT, SIR! THE GODS SAID TO *HELP* THEM!

NOW, NOW, MELLIE. SOME ORDERS TRANSCEND EVEN THE WISHES OF THE GODS. *ESPECIALLY* WHEN IT COMES TO THE FORCES OF NATURE.

WHAT'D I MISS?

JUST AEOLUS DECIDING THAT HE'S GOING TO KILL US.

FUMBLEROOSKI!

HOW TO KILL THEM...?

AHH!

?

WHOOSH

"--BEFORE IT'S TOO LATE."

GAEA.

WHERE ARE WE...?

WALNUT CREEK, CALIFORNIA. MELLIE SHOT US HALFWAY ACROSS THE COUNTRY.

WE WOULD'VE BEEN SMASHED FLAT, BUT SHE GAVE US A NICE SOFT BREEZE TO CUSHION OUR FALL.

I GOT YOU SOMETHING TO EAT.

THANKS. BUT AFTER THE DREAM I JUST HAD, I'M NOT HUNGRY.

GUYS, THE ENEMY WE'RE GOING UP AGAINST? THE ONE WHO LET MEDEA LOOSE ON THE EARTH AND SENT THOSE CYCLOPES RIGHT BACK FROM TARTARUS?

IT'S *GAEA*. WE'RE GOING HEAD-TO-HEAD AGAINST *MOTHER EARTH* HERSELF.

JASON? YOU REMEMBER SOMETHING, DON'T YOU? YOU'VE BEEN HERE BEFORE.

NO. OR MAYBE... YES.

IT JUST SEEMS IMPORTANT.

THAT'S *TITAN* LAND TO THE WEST. BELIEVE ME, WE'RE AS CLOSE TO 'FRISCO AS WE WANT TO GET.

NEVER MIND SAN FRANCISCO. I'M WORRIED ABOUT *HERE*.

HOW ARE WE GOING TO FIND PIPER'S DAD?

SMOKE EQUALS FIRE.

WE'D BETTER HURRY--

"--BEFORE IT BECOMES A *COOKING* FIRE."

IT'S FOUR AGAINST ONE. THIS IS GOING TO BE A PIECE OF CAKE.

DID YOU MISS THE PART WHERE HE'S *TWENTY FEET* TALL?

OKAY, SO THE THREE GUYS CHARGE STRAIGHT AT HIM WHILE PIPER SNEAKS AROUND TO FREE HER DAD.

I HATE TO SAY IT, BUT COACH IS RIGHT. A DISTRACTION IS PIPER'S BEST BET.

NOT A *SURE* BET. NOT EVEN A *GOOD* BET. JUST OUR *BEST* BET.

GREAT. LET'S GO, BEFORE I COME TO MY SENSES.

WHUP WHUP WHUP

YO! HOW ABOUT A LIFT?

WHUP WHUP WHUP

WHAT'RE YOU KIDS DOING HERE? YOU START THESE FIRES?

YOU DON'T SEE ANY FIRES.

AND YOU WON'T MIND TAKING US TO OAKLAND AIRPORT, EITHER.

I DON'T SEE...ANY FIRES.

I WON'T MIND...TAKING YOU TO OAKLAND AIRPORT.

PIPER, THEY TOLD ME YOU WOULD DIE...

THEY SAID TERRIBLE THINGS WERE GOING TO HAPPEN.

IT'S OKAY NOW, DAD. YOU'RE SAFE.

WE'RE GOING TO KEEP YOU SAFE.

THEY SAID YOU WERE A DEMIGOD. THEY SAID YOUR MOTHER WAS...

APHRODITE. GODDESS OF LOVE.

I DIDN'T KNOW UNTIL A FEW DAYS AGO. BUT IT'S TRUE. I ACTUALLY SPOKE TO MOM THIS MORNING. SHE SAID SHE STILL CARES ABOUT YOU.

AND I BELIEVE HER.

OH, GOD...SHE NEVER TOLD ME. WHY DIDN'T SHE TELL ME?

NOW I WISH I DIDN'T KNOW. THE THINGS I'VE SEEN...THE VISIONS THAT MONSTER SHOWED ME. HORRIBLE THINGS...

I COULDN'T BEAT THE MONSTER, BUT YOU DID. YOU'RE A HERO.

A REAL HERO. NOT A PRETENDER, LIKE ME...ACTING IN A MOVIE. I'M SO PROUD OF YOU. IT WAS WORTH IT--WORTH SEEING THOSE UNSPEAKABLE THINGS-- TO SEE THE PERSON YOU'VE BECOME.

DAD, DRINK THIS. IT'S... MEDICINE.

IT'LL MAKE YOU FEEL BETTER.

HORRIBLE THINGS...

SIP

SLEEP.

EVERYTHING WILL BE BETTER WHEN YOU WAKE UP.

WHAT WAS THAT?

I GOT IT FROM MY MOM. SHE SAID THE STRAIN OF EVERYTHING WOULD BE TOO MUCH FOR HIM. THE POTION WILL ERASE HIS RECENT MEMORIES. WHEN HE WAKES UP, HE WON'T REMEMBER ANY OF THIS.

HE WON'T REMEMBER THAT HE WAS EVER PROUD OF ME. I'LL GO BACK TO BEING THE *KLEPTOMANIAC* DAUGHTER WHO GETS *KICKED OUT* OF SCHOOLS.

~sob~

HEY, IT'S ALL RIGHT. WE STILL KNOW YOU'RE A HERO. THE WAY YOU STOOD UP TO ENCELADUS. THE WAY YOU STUCK BY YOUR FRIENDS, NO MATTER WHAT.

MAYBE YOUR DAD WON'T REMEMBER, BUT THAT DOESN'T MAKE IT ANY LESS REAL.

~sniff~
THANKS, GUYS. THANKS FOR EVERYTHING.

NO PROBLEM. DID YOUR MOM HAPPEN TO GIVE YOU A POTION THAT *RECOVERS* MEMORIES?

WE NEED AMNESIA BOY TO TELL US WHERE TO GO NEXT.

RIGHT, PAL?

"JASON?"

THAT ROAD. WHERE DOES IT GO?

THAT'S HIGHWAY 24. IT LEADS TO THE WOLF HOUSE. IT'S AN IMPORTANT PLACE FOR DEMIGODS.

THE *WOLF HOUSE?*

JACK LONDON BUILT IT BACK IN THE EARLY TWENTIETH CENTURY. HE WAS A HALF-BLOOD SON OF HERMES.

HE TRAVELED THE WORLD, THEN MADE A FORTUNE WRITING ABOUT IT.

THE WOLF HOUSE IS ON SACRED GROUND. JACKIE THOUGHT HE COULD CLAIM THE LAND AS HIS OWN, BUT IT WASN'T MEANT FOR HIM.

THE MANSION IS *CURSED.* IT BURNED TO THE GROUND A FEW WEEKS BEFORE HE AND HIS WIFE WERE SUPPOSED TO MOVE IN, AND JACKIE DIED A FEW YEARS LATER. HIS ASHES WERE BURIED ON THE SITE.

IT'S A POWERFUL PLACE.

HOW POWERFUL? POWERFUL ENOUGH TO IMPRISON HERA? TO RAISE PORPHYRION?

pfft--AS EASY AS RUNNING THROUGH WET TOILET PAPER. PROBABLY POWERFUL ENOUGH TO FULLY *AWAKEN* THE EARTH GODDESS.

JASON, YOU DON'T THINK...?

IT'S THE PLACE I SAW IN MY DREAMS. IT *HAS* TO BE.

CAN YOU TELL THE PILOT--?

WAY AHEAD OF YOU.

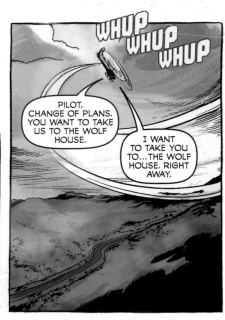

WHUP WHUP WHUP

PILOT, CHANGE OF PLANS. YOU WANT TO TAKE US TO THE WOLF HOUSE.

I WANT TO TAKE YOU TO...THE WOLF HOUSE. RIGHT AWAY.

LATER.

WHUP
WHUP
WHUP

AN *ICE STORM?* IS IT SUPPOSED TO GET THIS COLD AROUND HERE?

I'M NOT SURE, BUT I KNOW WE'RE GETTING CLOSE.

PILOT, START BRINGING US DOWN.

I HAVE NO IDEA WHAT WE'RE FLYING INTO. IT MIGHT NOT BE SAFE FOR YOUR DAD.

WHAT DO YOU WANT TO DO?

HE AND I CAN LEAVE WITH THE CHOPPER. I'LL MAKE SURE HE GETS HOME.

WHAT? I'M UP TO THE CHALLENGE. WE SATYRS HAVE A LONG TRADITION OF BEING PROTECTORS.

BESIDES, I'VE BEEN SHOWING YOU GUYS MY BEST *FIGHT MOVES* SINCE PIKES PEAK. IF YOU WERE PAYING ATTENTION, YOU'LL BE ABLE TO FEND FOR YOURSELVES.

-*snicker*- FIGHT MOVES--?

ABSOLUTELY, COACH. WE'LL MISS YOU ON THE BATTLEFIELD. YOU'VE BEEN AN INSPIRATION.

WHUP WHUP WHUP

BYE, DAD. I LOVE YOU. I'LL SEE YOU SOON.

DON'T WORRY, KID. HE'LL BE IN GOOD HANDS.

REMEMBER, THE BEST DEFENSE IS A GOOD *OFFENSE*!

WHUP WHUP WHUP

...THIS IS IT.

THE HOUSE IN YOUR DREAMS?

YEAH, BUT IT'S MORE THAN THAT....

BEING HERE IS BRINGING BACK MEMORIES. THIS IS WHERE MY MOM TOOK ME AND THALIA WHEN WE WERE KIDS. SHE LEFT ME HERE.

BECAUSE HERA *TOLD* HER TO.

SPEAKING OF HERA...LET'S SPRING HER FROM JAIL AND GET OUT OF HERE. I DON'T LIKE THE LOOKS OF THIS PLACE.

SHE SHOULD BE IN THE COURTYARD. BY THE REFLECTING POOL.

THIS WAY.

THREE GUESSES WHO'S INSIDE THE GIANT DIRT PIÑATA.

PORPHYRION. IT'S ALMOST SUNDOWN. WE SHOULD HURRY.

YES. YOU SHOULD.

HERA.

HOLA, TÍA CALLIDA. LONG TIME NO SEE.

DON'T INSPECT ME LIKE ONE OF YOUR MACHINES, LEO VALDEZ. RELEASE ME!

IT IS GOOD TO SEE YOU AGAIN, JASON. I CHOSE MY CHAMPION WELL.

I'M NOT YOUR *CHAMPION*, LADY.

I'M ONLY HELPING YOU BECAUSE YOU'RE BETTER THAN THE ALTERNATIVE.

INDEED I AM. PORPHYRION IS NEARLY REBORN.

GAEA NEEDED A GREAT DEAL OF POWER TO RAISE HIM AGAIN.

MY POWER. FOR WEEKS I HAVE GROWN WEAKER AS MY ESSENCE WAS DRAINED TO GROW THE GIANT KING A NEW FORM.

AT SUNDOWN, HE WILL AWAKE. HE WILL OFFER ME A *CHOICE*: TO MARRY HIM, OR TO BE CONSUMED BY THE EARTH...AND I CANNOT MARRY HIM.

WE WILL ALL BE DESTROYED, AND AS WE DIE *GAEA* WILL AWAKEN.

WAIT. WHERE'S THALIA?

WE WERE SUPPOSED TO MEET HER HERE.

HAVE YOU SEEN THE HUNTERS?

YOUR SISTER WAS NOT THE *ONLY* ONE WAITING FOR YOU, SON OF ZEUS.

SHE GREW IMPATIENT--

I HAVE.

--SO I PUT HER *ON ICE*.

I'VE BEEN WANTING TO SHUT YOU UP FOR *MILLENNIA*.

ONLY A FEW MOMENTS LONGER. THE SUN WILL SET, PORPHYRION WILL RISE. AND YOU WILL BE *QUIET* AT LAST.

THEN WE WILL RETAKE THE ANCIENT PLACES OF EARTH AND DESTROY THE ROOTS OF THE GODS. I WILL *PERSONALLY* BURY THE ACROPOLIS IN SNOW.

OLYMPUS WILL NOT JUST FALL. IT WILL BE GONE. *FOREVER.*

I CAN'T BELIEVE I EVER THOUGHT YOU WERE HOT.

HOT? YOU DARE INSULT ME? I AM VERY, *VERY* COLD.

IT'S TIME YOU LEARNED HOW COLD.

KILL THE DEMIGODS!

LET THEM BE KING PORPHYRION'S FIRST MEAL!

GROWL

GROWL

IF YOU WERE *HALF* AS SMART AS YOU ARE TALL, YOU'D BE WORRIED ABOUT *ME*, NOT MY FATHER.

I HOPE YOU ENJOY YOUR *TWO MINUTES* OF REBIRTH, GIANT, BECAUSE I'M GOING TO SEND YOU RIGHT BACK TO TARTARUS.

TALK DOES NOT FRIGHTEN ME. I WILL TAKE YOUR FATHER'S THRONE. I WILL TAKE HIS *WIFE*--OR, IF SHE WILL NOT HAVE ME, I WILL LET THE EARTH CONSUME HER LIFE FORCE.

WHAT YOU SEE BEFORE YOU IS ONLY MY WEAKENED FORM. I WILL GROW STRONGER BY THE HOUR, UNTIL I AM *INVINCIBLE!*

SHRRRR

HURRY!

THIS IS ME HURRYING!

HOW ABOUT A NAP, CAGE?

YOU MUST BE SO-O-O *TIRED*.

SWOOSH

MIND IF I BORROW THIS?

WHAT WAS *THAT*?

I UNLEASHED MY POWER.

I BECAME *PURE ENERGY*, SO I COULD DISINTEGRATE THE MONSTERS AND RESTORE THIS PLACE.

"*DEATH UNLEASH, THROUGH HERA'S RAGE.*"

JUST LIKE THE ORACLE SAID.

SO THAT'S IT? PORPHYRION IS DEAD?

WE WON?

HARDLY.

A GIANT CAN ONLY BE KILLED BY A COMBINATION OF GOD AND DEMIGOD, WORKING TOGETHER.

BY SAVING ME, YOU PREVENTED GAEA FROM WAKING. YOU HAVE BOUGHT US SOME TIME.

BUT PORPHYRION IS RISEN. HE WILL REGAIN HIS FULL POWER, AND REFOCUS IT ON THE *TRUE* PRIZE.

GREECE.

IF HE DESTROYS THE ANCIENT PLACES, THE GODS WILL CEASE TO EXIST.

THERE'LL BE *NOTHING* TO TETHER THEM TO THIS WORLD.

THALIA! YOU'RE *ALIVE*!

YEAH, LITTLE BROTHER. STILL KIND OF COLD, BUT ALIVE.

THANKS TO *YOU*.

AND NOW WE HAVE TO SEPARATE AGAIN. I HAVE TO FIND ANNABETH AND TELL HER WHAT'S HAPPENED. SHE NEEDS TO KNOW ABOUT PORPHYRION.

I'LL CATCH UP WITH YOU BACK AT CAMP HALF-BLOOD. HERA CAN GET YOU THERE.

I WANT *ANSWERS* FIRST. I REMEMBER SOME STUFF, BUT NOT EVERYTHING.

MY MOM LEFT ME AT THIS HOUSE WHEN I WAS TWO, BUT WHERE HAVE I BEEN SINCE?

TO GIVE YOU THE ANSWERS WOULD BE TO RENDER THOSE ANSWERS INVALID.

THAT IS THE WAY OF THE FATES.

YOU MUST FIND YOUR OWN DESTINY. AND WHEN YOU DO, YOU WILL UNITE TWO *GREAT POWERS*. YOU WILL GIVE US HOPE AGAINST THE GIANTS--AND GAEA HERSELF.

THAT IS ALL I CAN SAY. I WILL RETURN YOU TO CAMP HALF-BLOOD, WHERE YOU WILL BEGIN PREPARING FOR THE NEXT PHASE.

YOU HAVE DONE ME A GREAT SERVICE, MY HEROES.

"FAREWELL."

WAKE UP!

YOU'RE GOING TO MAKE US LATE FOR BREAKFAST, WHICH MEANS *YOU* GET TO CLEAN THE CABIN FOR INSPECTION.

NO, DREW.

YOU DON'T GET TO *BOSS* PEOPLE AROUND ANYMORE.

W-WHAT ARE YOU DOING...?

CHALLENGING YOU.

I'M NOT AFRAID OF YOU. AND I DON'T MUCH *CARE* FOR THE WAY YOU RUN THE APHRODITE CABIN, EITHER.

APHRODITE ISN'T JUST ABOUT LOVE AND BEAUTY. SHE'S ABOUT *BEING* LOVING. *SPREADING* BEAUTY.

YOU DO *NEITHER*.

CAMP RULES SAY I CAN CHALLENGE YOU, IF I FEEL I CAN DO A BETTER JOB. HOW ABOUT NOON IN THE ARENA? YOU CAN CHOOSE THE WEAPONS. NOT THAT IT'LL MATTER--I'VE FOUGHT *WAY* TOUGHER OPPONENTS.

OF COURSE, YOU CAN ALWAYS *STEP DOWN*, IF YOU'RE NOT UP FOR IT.

YOU WANT TO BE SENIOR COUNSELOR? *FINE*. HAVE FUN LEADING THIS GROUP OF LOSERS.

BUT DON'T THINK I'M GOING TO FORGET THIS, MCLEAN.

OH, I HOPE YOU DON'T.

AND WHILE YOU'RE AT IT, REMEMBER *THIS*, TOO:

HE MAY NOT KNOW IT YET, BUT JASON IS *MINE*. YOU SO MUCH AS LOOK AT HIM, I'LL LOAD YOU INTO A CATAPULT AND SHOOT YOU ACROSS LONG ISLAND SOUND.

SLAM!

SO...

YOU GUYS WANT TO PITCH IN AND GET THE CABIN READY FOR INSPECTION... *TOGETHER*?

WE LIKE YOU BETTER ALREADY!

I WISH I COULD TALK TO YOU IN PERSON... BUT I UNDERSTAND YOU CAN'T DO THAT.

THE ROMAN GODS DON'T LIKE TO INTERACT WITH MORTALS SO MUCH, AND...WELL, YOU'RE THE *KING*. YOU HAVE TO SET AN EXAMPLE.

I REMEMBER SOME THINGS. LIKE THAT IT'S HARD BEING THE SON OF JUPITER.

EVERYONE IS ALWAYS LOOKING TO ME TO BE THE LEADER, LIKE I SOMEHOW MAGICALLY KNOW EVERYTHING.

I DON'T KNOW HOW TO PROTECT MY FRIENDS, THOUGH. I'M AFRAID I'M GOING TO GET THEM KILLED.

I COULD REALLY USE SOME GUIDANCE, DAD.

YOUR FRIENDS *ARE* YOUR GUIDANCE, MY CHAMPION.

YOUR FATHER SENT YOU PIPER AND LEO.

LISTEN TO THEM, AND YOU'LL DO WELL.

I DIDN'T ASK TO BE A PART OF THIS. WHY DID YOU SEND ME TO THIS CAMP?

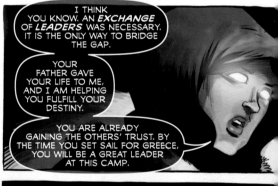

I THINK YOU KNOW. AN *EXCHANGE* OF *LEADERS* WAS NECESSARY. IT IS THE ONLY WAY TO BRIDGE THE GAP.

YOUR FATHER GAVE YOUR LIFE TO ME, AND I AM HELPING YOU FULFILL YOUR DESTINY.

YOU ARE ALREADY GAINING THE OTHERS' TRUST. BY THE TIME YOU SET SAIL FOR GREECE, YOU WILL BE A GREAT LEADER AT THIS CAMP.

GREECE? YOU WANT ME TO GO TO *GREECE*?

YES. BUT BEFORE YOU GO, YOU MUST UNITE TWO POWERFUL FORCES.

IF THEY REMAIN DIVIDED, THE GIANTS WILL SURELY WIN. GAEA IS COUNTING ON THIS.

FAIL, AND THERE WILL BE **BLOODSHED** LIKE WE HAVE NEVER SEEN. DEMIGODS WILL DESTROY ONE ANOTHER. THE GIANTS WILL OVERRUN OLYMPUS.

GAEA WILL WAKE, AND THE EARTH WILL SHAKE OFF EVERYTHING WE HAVE BUILT OVER FIVE MILLENNIA.

IT WILL BE THE END OF US ALL.

AND IF I FAIL?

TAKE THIS, TO REPLACE THE WEAPON YOU LOST. AND HAVE COURAGE.

LIKE IT OR NOT, JASON, I AM YOUR SPONSOR, AND YOUR LINK TO OLYMPUS. I WILL BE WITH YOU.

KNOCK KNOCK

WHAT ABOUT--?

HELLO?

JUNO?

HEY.

PIPER! COME ON IN.

YOU TALK TO YOUR DAD? HOW'S HE DOING?

HE'S GREAT. REALLY GREAT. TURNS OUT HIS ASSISTANT, JANE--WHO I *NEVER* LIKED, BY THE WAY--WAS WORKING FOR MEDEA.

THAT'S HOW MY DAD ENDED UP GOING TO MOUNT DIABLO WITHOUT ANYONE KNOWING. HE THOUGHT HE WAS SHOOTING A COMMERCIAL FOR A CHARITY.

DAD THINKS COACH HEDGE IS A *LIFE* COACH, AND HE'S HIRED HIM ON STAFF.

ALONG WITH MELLIE, THE AURA WHO HELPED US ESCAPE AEOLUS.

SHE'S DAD'S NEW ASSISTANT.

ANYWAY, HE DOESN'T REMEMBER ANYTHING, BUT HE'S SAFE. THAT'S THE IMPORTANT THING.

I'M REALLY HAPPY FOR YOU, PIPER.

SO, HOW ARE YOU? ANY MORE MEMORIES COMING BACK?

YEAH. UNFORTUNATELY, THEY AREN'T GOOD.

FOR *ANY* OF US.

IT'LL ALL WORK OUT. YOU'RE GOING TO LEAD US, JASON. I'D FOLLOW YOU ANYWHERE.

THAT'S A DANGEROUS THING TO SAY.

I'M A DANGEROUS GIRL.

THAT, I BELIEVE.

~ahem~ CHIRON HAS CALLED A MEETING WITH US AND SOME OF THE SENIOR COUNSELORS. HE SAYS LEO HAS SOMETHING TO SHOW US IN THE WOODS.

YOU COMING?

LEAD THE WAY.

"I'D FOLLOW YOU ANYWHERE."

THANKS FOR COMING, YOU GUYS.

THIS BETTER BE GOOD.

CHIRON CALLED ME BACK TO CAMP, EVEN THOUGH I *STILL* HAVEN'T FOUND PERCY.

LEO! YOU'RE A *FIRE USER*!

YOU THINK?

HOLY HEPHAESTUS. THAT'S SO RARE...

WELCOME TO BUNKER NINE.

IT'S FESTUS. HE'S MEANT TO BE OUR MASTHEAD. OUR GOOD LUCK CHARM, OUR EYES AT SEA.

I'M SUPPOSED TO BUILD THIS SHIP. I'M GOING TO CALL IT THE *ARGO II*, AFTER THE ORIGINAL JASON'S SHIP. AND I NEED YOUR HELP.

NOT YET, BUT IT *WILL* BE.

LOOK AT THE MASTHEAD.

SOMETHING ISN'T ADDING UP. THIS IS A *WARTIME* COMMAND CENTER. IT'S BEEN UNDER OUR NOSES ALL THIS TIME, BUT NO ONE KNEW ABOUT IT?

HOW'D IT GET HERE, THEN?

CHIRON?

THE LAST TIME THIS PLACE WAS USED WAS DURING THE CIVIL WAR.

THE *AMERICAN* CIVIL WAR? LIKE, IN 1864?

YES AND NO. THE TWO CONFLICTS-- MORTAL AND DEMIGOD-- MIRRORED EACH OTHER, AS THEY SO OFTEN DO IN WESTERN HISTORY.

LOOK AT ANY CIVIL WAR OR REVOLUTION SINCE THE FALL OF ROME, AND IT MARKS A TIME WHEN DEMIGODS ALSO FOUGHT EACH OTHER.

BUT THE 1860S WERE AN *AWFUL* TIME.

EVEN THEN, CAMP HALF-BLOOD WAS HERE. A BATTLE RAGED IN THESE WOODS FOR DAYS.

WHEN THE WAR WAS ENDED, THE GODS WERE SO HORRIFIED BY THE TOLL IT TOOK ON THEIR CHILDREN, THEY SWORE IT WOULD NEVER HAPPEN AGAIN.

THEY BENT THEIR WILL, WOVE THE MISTS AS *TIGHTLY* AS THEY COULD, TO ENSURE THE TWO SIDES WOULD NEVER KNOW EACH OTHER EXISTED.

EVEN DURING THE TITAN WAR, WHEN KRONOS'S ARMIES THREATENED CAMP, I DID NOT THINK IT WORTH THE *RISK* TO REVEAL THIS PLACE.

TWO SIDES. YOU MEAN CAMP HALF-BLOOD SPLIT APART?

WHO WAS THE OTHER SIDE?

NO. HE MEANS CAMP HALF-BLOOD WAS ONLY *ONE* SIDE IN THE WAR.

ROMANS.

THAT'S IT, ISN'T IT? THERE'S ANOTHER CAMP SOMEWHERE WITH HALF-BLOOD CHILDREN OF THE ROMAN GODS.

LIKE *ME.*

YES. BUT DO NOT ASK ME WHERE. EVEN I HAVE NEVER BEEN TRUSTED WITH THAT INFORMATION.

LUPA, MY COUNTERPART, IS NOT EXACTLY THE SHARING TYPE.

THEN IT'S SETTLED. WE HAVE TO FIND IT.

THE GREAT PROPHECY SAID SEVEN DEMIGODS WILL BE NEEDED TO DEFEAT THE GIANTS. AND HERA TOLD ME THAT SHE SENT ME HERE TO HELP UNITE TWO GREAT POWERS.

SHE MEANS THE TWO *CAMPS*.

THE GREEK AND ROMAN CAMPS HAVE TO JOIN FORCES, AND FIND A WAY TO GET ALONG.

WHEN DO WE LEAVE?

YOU KNOW THERE'S *NO WAY* I'M NOT GOING WITH YOU.

I WAS HOPING YOU'D SAY THAT. OF ALL PEOPLE, WE NEED *YOU* MOST.

WHY HER? I MEAN, I'M COOL WITH ANNABETH GOING, BUT WHAT MAKES HER SO SPECIAL?

HERA SAID MY COMING HERE WAS AN EXCHANGE OF LEADERS. A WAY FOR THE TWO CAMPS TO LEARN OF EACH OTHER'S EXISTENCE.

AN EXCHANGE GOES *TWO* WAYS.

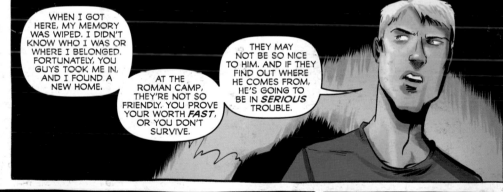

WHEN I GOT HERE, MY MEMORY WAS WIPED. I DIDN'T KNOW WHO I WAS OR WHERE I BELONGED. FORTUNATELY, YOU GUYS TOOK ME IN, AND I FOUND A NEW HOME.

AT THE ROMAN CAMP, THEY'RE NOT SO FRIENDLY. YOU PROVE YOUR WORTH *FAST*, OR YOU DON'T SURVIVE.

THEY MAY NOT BE SO NICE TO HIM. AND IF THEY FIND OUT WHERE HE COMES FROM, HE'S GOING TO BE IN *SERIOUS* TROUBLE.

HIM? WHO'S HIM?

MY BOYFRIEND.

HE DISAPPEARED AROUND THE SAME TIME JASON APPEARED. IF JASON CAME TO CAMP HALF-BLOOD--

EXACTLY.

PERCY JACKSON IS AT THE *OTHER* CAMP--

HEROES OF OLYMPUS
THE LOST HERO

THE GRAPHIC NOVEL

by

RICK RIORDAN

Adapted by
ROBERT VENDITTI

Art by
NATE POWELL

Colour by
ORPHEUS COLLAR

Lettering by
CHRIS DICKEY

PUFFIN BOOKS

Published by the Penguin Group: London, New York, Australia,
Canada, India, Ireland, New Zealand and South Africa
Penguin Books Ltd, Registered Offices: 80 Strand, London WC2R 0RL, England

puffinbooks.com

Adapted from the novel *Heroes of Olympus: The Lost Hero*,
published in Great Britain by Puffin Books
Graphic novel first published in USA by Disney•Hyperion Books,
an imprint of Disney Book Group, 2014
Published simultaneously in Great Britain by Puffin Books 2014
001

Text copyright © Rick Riordan, 2014
Illustrations copyright © Disney Enterprises, Inc., 2014
Design by Jim Titus
The moral right of the author and illustrator has been asserted
All rights reserved

Made and printed in Italy by Printer Trento Srl

British Library Cataloguing in Publication Data
A CIP catalogue record for this book is available from the British Library

ISBN: 978-0-141-35998-4